SINFUL UNION

AN AGE GAP, BRATVA ROMANCE

K.C. CROWNE

Copyright © 2025 by K.C. Crowne

All rights reserved.

No part of this book may be reproduced in any form or by any electronic or mechanical means, including information storage and retrieval systems, without written permission from the author, except for the use of brief quotations in a book review.

DESCRIPTION

"Smile for me, malyshka."
His voice cracks through the chapel like a whip.

Six years ago, Pavel Fetisov ruined me.
The Bratva king who stole my innocence against these cursed walls now slides a blood diamond onto my finger.

They say his family killed my parents.
Now, my brothers want his empire in ashes.

But Pavel isn't just powerful.
He's ruthless. Obsessive. Addicted to control.
And every brush of his hands burns through my hatred.

He doesn't know.
That in the shadows, *a little girl waits*—
With his eyes.
With his unshakable will.
With his blood in her veins.

The plan was perfect.
Until I started falling for the devil himself.

One deadly truth will destroy us both:
The Bratva don doesn't forgive.
And he *never* forgets.

Readers note: This is full-length standalone, secret baby, Russian bratva, age-gap, romantic suspense. K.C. Crowne is an Amazon Top 6 Bestseller and International Bestselling Author.

CHAPTER 1

KAT

*My fiancé will get his climax on our wedding night...
Just not the one he's expecting.*

Courtney adjusts my veil. The same antique lace that once crowned my mother's head, now framing mine. How fitting.

"God, you're stunning," she gushes, stepping back to admire her handiwork. "If your man sees you like this, he'll rip that dress off before you even say 'I do'."

She giggles, blissfully unaware of the poison vial I've just tucked into my bouquet. The vial bites into my palm, its contents thick as regret.

If only she knew.

The gown is everything I once dreamed about: ivory silk that molds to the curves Pavel used to trace like scripture, pearls sewn into the bodice with surgical precision.

Courtney spins me toward the mirror. "Well? Do we love it?"

"I-It's perfect," I breathe, pulse thudding against the hidden vial.

Piotr's voice slithers through my mind: Marry Pavel Fetisov. Earn his trust. Finish the job.

Easy enough—except for the killing-my-ex-first-love part. I remember Pavel's laugh, the way he'd tug me close and murmur solnyshko—his little sunshine—like I was something precious. All lies in the end.

The Fetisovs stole everything from us.

I'm not a killer. But tonight, I'll kneel at an altar and lie to a man I once loved. And when he kisses me, I'll taste vengeance on my tongue.

Six years ago, I thought Pavel was my future.

I loved him in that reckless, all-consuming way only first love can be—trusted him with my secrets, my body, the jagged pieces of my soul he promised to keep safe. He kissed my scars and called them beautiful. Held me after the funeral when I sobbed for parents I didn't yet know *he'd* helped bury.

Piotr revealed the truth. He told me Pavel and the rest of the Fetisov Bratva orchestrated our parents' deaths.

I immediately ended it. That night, I crushed everything we'd built, and swore I'd never look back.

A few months later, I found out I was pregnant.

My daughter was the best damn thing that could ever happen to me.

Ofcourse, Piotr didn't take the news well. Furious doesn't even begin to cover it. He sent me south to our Aunt Irena's estate, far away from prying eyes and any chance of the Fetisovs learning the truth. There, I gave birth to Ana, my beautiful, sweet girl, who deserves to live her best life, one not hidden in the shadows.

When we returned to the family home two months ago, I thought I'd feel a sense of relief. Instead, it feels like I've traded one cage for another. Piotr and I agreed that Ana's paternity must remain a secret.

Especially from Pavel.

As I gaze at my image in the mirror, I exhale slowly, trying to ignore the gnawing doubt at the back of my mind.

This is the right thing to do.

Pavel deserves this. His family deserves this. And yet…

Courtney takes a step back and looks me over one last time.

"Absolutely perfect," she says with one final approving nod. "Don't want to toot my own horn, but your dress might be my finest work so far."

"You've done an amazing job." I plaster a bright smile on my face, doing my best to look the part I'm playing.

But my mind's a million miles away.

Courtney studies my face, worry softening her smile. "Hey, you okay? I'm only the dress girl, but you look like you're carrying a whole lot more than lace right now."

"It's nothing, just last-minute butterflies," I say with a smile in a cheerful tone.

"Good." Her smile doesn't reach her eyes.

A soft knock at the door interrupts us. I turn, waiting for the person on the other side to speak.

"It's time." The deep, resonant voice of my other older brother, Vlad, comes through.

"I can tell him I'm not done yet, if you need a few more minutes," Courtney says.

The offer's tempting, but I shake my head.

"No, but thank you. Time to get this show on the road."

I steal one more glance at my reflection before turning and striding toward the door.

A petite, curvy bride stares back at me—long, straight brown hair cascading over bare shoulders, smoky brown eyes framed by arched brows, full lips set in determined silence.

She's stubborn. Strong-willed. Loyal to a fault. A devoted mother.

Not some simpering girl in a fairytale—

No.

She's a woman walking into hell with her chin held high... and a secret buried beneath ivory silk.

Vlad stands on the other side, his expression warm but serious. He has always been my anchor, my quiet support, when Piotr's fire becomes too overwhelming.

Vlad is tall, handsome, and solidly built, with the same blue eyes as our father. His dark hair is slicked back. He's dressed in a perfectly tailored tux, looking every bit the supportive brother.

He looks me over, his lips curving into a faint smile.

"You look beautiful," he says softly. "Mother would be proud."

"Don't start," I reply, waving him off with mock irritation.

He chuckles, holding out his arm. "Ready?"

Not even a little, but I take his arm, straightening my back. "As I'll ever be..."

We walk in silence for a moment, his presence grounding me. I know what's on his mind. Unlike Piotr, Vlad is totally against this plan.

He sighs heavily as we make our way through the halls of the church.

"You don't have to do this," he finally says.

"Yes, I do," I reply firmly.

He shakes his head. "I know your reasoning. And I know that Piotr has put pressure on you to—"

I pause, turning to him. "You think this is all Piotr's doing?" I ask, my voice low. "Like I'm some naive little girl who can't make my own decisions?"

Another sigh. "That's not what I meant."

"Then tell me what you meant."

"They'll kill you the second they suspect," Vlad growls, crushing my hand in his calloused grip. "Pavel's not some reckless boy in love anymore—he's the Pakhan now. He commands an army of killers. You think he'll hesitate to slit your throat the moment he senses betrayal?"

"I'm not afraid of him."

"You should be," he snaps. "You have no idea what he's become. The things he's done." His jaw ticks. "I've seen the bodies, sestra. Men tortured for less than a stray look. You step into that chapel, you're not walking down the aisle—you're walking into a den of wolves wearing white."

I swallow hard but don't let my voice shake. "You're not going to lose me."

"It's not your courage I doubt," he says, softer now, but no less intense. "You've always been the brave one. The stubborn one. But this... this is a suicide mission. And for what? To satisfy some—"

"This isn't about vengeance," I cut in sharply. "This is about survival. About protecting Ana."

Vlad flinches at her name.

"If Pavel finds out he has a daughter," I continue, voice low and trembling with fury, "he'll take her from me like she's a prize to claim. He'll raise her in that cold empire of his, mold her into one of them. She won't be safe. She won't be mine."

I look him dead in the eye. "You want to protect me? Then understand this: I'm not doing this for revenge. I'm doing it because if that man draws one more breath, everything I love stays in danger."

Vlad's eyes darken with a swirl of pain and pride. He reaches for me, pulling me into a tight embrace that smells of cedar and home. "I just... I've already lost too much, little sister. I can't lose you too."

His voice breaks on the last word.

I squeeze his hand, then cradle his cheek. "You won't. By this time next week, Pavel Fetisov will be rotting in the ground, and Ana will have the future she deserves. One where she's free."

He nods, though his throat works with the effort of holding back words he doesn't say. The doubt lingers in his eyes, but he lets me go.

"Come on," I whisper, straightening my spine. "You've got a sister to give away."

A faint, bitter smile tugs at his lips. "Yeah... to a monster."

"To his execution," I correct softly. "He just doesn't know it yet."

And with that, we walk toward the chapel—where vows will be spoken, secrets buried, and blood, if needed, will be spilled.

I grip Vlad's arm tightly as we step into the hallway, my nerves twisting into a tight, merciless knot. My stomach churns, threatening to rebel, but I hold my head high. Despite my tough talk, I am scared.

My brother is right. There are all sorts of ways this plan could go awry.

But this is no time for weakness, not when I'm walking into the lion's den, wrapped in white satin, pretending to be a willing lamb.

Vlad's presence is steady beside me, his hand resting lightly over mine.

When we reach the entrance to the chapel, I pause. My grip tightens on Vlad's arm. A faint murmur of voices filters through the wooden doors, and my breath hitches.

"It's time," Vlad says quietly. "It's not too late, you know. You could still play runaway bride and vanish into the wind." A dry chuckle escapes him. "I'll just tell everyone I tried to stop you."

Despite the storm inside me, I manage a faint smile.

"No. I'm seeing this through."

He nods slowly, his eyes scanning my face like he's memorizing it. Like he's afraid it's the last time he'll see me whole.

"Well then..." he says, voice tight with emotion. "Good luck, sestra."

He rests a hand over mine—one last, silent plea for safety—

Then turns and pushes the chapel doors open.

And just like that, there's no turning back.

The chapel is grand—vaulted ceilings, sunlight pouring through stained glass like blessings I don't deserve. But only one side of the pews is full.

My side, the Andreevs, is a ghost town. Most of my family refused to attend, unwilling to witness what they see as treason wrapped in lace.

The Fetisovs are here in full force. A silent wall of dark hair and ice-blue eyes. Predators dressed in designer suits. Their gazes pin me in place like I'm already prey.

Then I see him. At the alter.

Pavel doesn't move as I walk. He never does.

His stillness is its own kind of violence—controlled, calculating, absolute.

The room bends around his gravity, as if every soul inside knows: nothing happens here unless he allows it.

Standing tall—calm, confident, dangerous. Power clings to him like a second skin.

His suit fits like sin, the rich fabric hugging broad shoulders and tapering over a body I still remember too well. His dark hair is laced with silver now, a cruel evolution that only sharpens his appeal.

His jaw flexes when he sees me.

It's subtle—so fast I almost miss it—but it's there.

A shadow of something old. Pain. Possession. Loss.

Then it's gone, replaced with that familiar mask of cold command.

A wave of heat rises in me—sharp, shameful.

My thighs clench.

God, not now.

I hate the way my body remembers his.

How he once moved inside me, slow then brutal, a rhythm designed to ruin.

How he whispered filth in Russian while I came undone in his arms.

Six years.

Six years, and my body still burns for the man who destroyed my life.

Beside him, Piotr plays the role of devoted ally, smiling at the man he's marked for death.

His mask is flawless, a performance honed over years of lies and shared vodka toasts.

I grip Vlad's hand like a lifeline.

"You good?" he asks, voice low, tense.

"I'm fine," I lie.

I force my gaze away from Pavel—to the high arches, the flowers, anything but him.

But I can feel it.

The heat of his stare dragging over my skin like a promise.

My pulse stutters.

Anger blooms in my chest.

Why couldn't time have ravaged him?

Why does he have to look like sin dipped in silk?

Why does he still smell like cedar and winter and ruin?

This is the man who stole my parents.

The man who made me a mother in hiding.

He should repulse me.

But my body—traitorous and weak—wants him still.

As we reach the altar, Vlad releases my arm. His fingers linger for just a beat longer than necessary before he steps aside.

Pavel's eyes lock onto mine.

My knees wobble beneath the weight of his gaze.

There's something in his eyes I can't place—something old.

Like he's lived a thousand lives and buried all of them.

Or maybe it's just regret, twisted into something cold and sharp.

"Kat," he says.

His voice is low and rough—gravel and smoke. It slices right through me.

Damn him.

Damn me.

He threads his fingers through mine, the gesture intimate—claiming. A snare wrapped in affection. I refuse to look away.

His expression is unreadable, but there's a flicker in his eyes—a smirk tugging at the corner of his mouth.

Arrogant bastard. He thinks he still owns me.

The officiant begins to speak, but the words blur, meaningless.

All I can feel is the warm pressure of his hand in mine...

And the maddening graze of his thumb across my palm.

It's soft. Repetitive. Designed to disarm.

It works.

Heat coils low in my belly.

No.

I steel my spine.

Remember.

My parents.

Ana.

The years I spent living like a ghost while he built his empire.

Then, Pavel leans in, breath warm against my cheek.

"You're breathtaking, Malyshka," he murmurs. "I've imagined you in white for six years.."

His thumb drags slowly across my palm—reverent, possessive—like he's reacquainting himself with sacred ground.

I squeeze his hand tighter. Let him think it's longing. Let him think I'm still his.

The deeper he falls back into this fantasy—

The easier it'll be to slip the poison past his lips.

CHAPTER 2

PAVEL

The years have only made her more dangerous.

More beautiful.

More woman.

She was always stunning, but now?

Now she's devastating.

Curves that were once soft with youth have ripened into something feral and feminine—full hips, a narrow waist, thighs that could crush a man's resolve. She isn't some waifish doll men parade around like trophies.

She's real. Solid. Built like sin and meant to be worshipped.

My ideal.

And she's standing in front of me in a dress that clings to every inch of her like it was sewn by the devil himself.

How the fuck am I supposed to focus on the priest when she looks like that?

"Blessed is the kingdom of the Father, and of the Son, and of the Holy Spirit..."

My eyes rake down her body—slow, hungry.

The silk hugs her like a secret I want to unravel. The lace teases just enough of her full breasts to drive me insane, and the dip of her waist flares into hips that were made to be gripped, to be held down, to carry my child.

She's not just beautiful.

She's fucking mine.

"Let us pray to the Lord..."

I remember her body under me six years ago—warm, flushed, trembling.

I remember how it felt to bury myself inside her, her thighs wrapped around me, her moans like music I still dream about.

The way she arched when she came, her nails carving into my skin like she was afraid I'd disappear.

No one's ever matched her. No one ever could.

And no matter how much time has passed, I know she remembers too.

"O Lord, bless this union as Thou didst bless Cana of Galilee..."

Her hair tumbles down her back in soft waves, a dark halo against the white of her gown. But it's her eyes that kill me— those deep, smoky eyes that flash with fire and defiance when they meet mine.

She looks away too quickly.

But I saw it.

Recognition. Memory. That ache neither of us has outrun.

She's still angry. Still proud.

Still the strongest woman I've ever known.

Good.

Because I don't want some fragile thing I can break.

I want her.

All of her.

The fire. The fight. The curves. The soul.

And before this night is over, she'll remember exactly what she means to me.

Not just a body I crave.

But the woman I've never stopped wanting.

The only one I've ever needed.

"O Lord our God, who hast espoused the Church as a pure virgin, bless this betrothal..."

My expression remains cold, unreadable. But inside, my blood is boiling. Something I've spent six goddamn years trying to forget grips me. I thought this was over. I thought I had buried every last piece of what she once made me feel.

I was wrong.

"The servant of God, Pavel, is betrothed to the servant of God, Katerina, in the name of the Father, and of the Son, and of the Holy Spirit."

When Piotr first proposed this marriage, I almost laughed in his face. The idea that I would take back the woman who disappeared from my life without a word, that I would tie myself to someone who walked away from me like I meant nothing, was almost insulting.

But now, as she stands before me, every bit the beautiful, blushing bride, all I can think is—*why?*

There's still something here. Something raw, something unresolved.

"Grant unto them a long life of mutual love in the bond of peace..."

I tear my gaze away from her long enough to glance at Piotr. He's standing beside me, his expression the perfect display of brotherly affection as he regards his sister. But when his gaze shifts to me, something dark flickers in his eyes.

"Fill their hearts with love for one another..."

The small, pleased smile on his lips widens as he nods at me, the picture of a loyal friend, a brother welcoming me into the family.

But it feels fake. Something is off.

"May the Lord bless and keep them from all harm..."

Vlad and Piotr, the Andreev brothers, came to me weeks ago, talking of alliances, of power, of finally eliminating the Novikov Bratva and solidifying our hold on the city. On paper, the deal makes sense. Once we merge our families, the Novikovs won't stand a chance.

All it would take is a marriage to their beautiful sister to make it official. She and I have history; therefore, it would make sense for us to officially become husband and wife.

But why now?

"May the Lord grant unto them peace, harmony, and love eternal..."

For years, there's been nothing but bad blood between us. The larger Andreev family blamed my family for their parents' deaths, in the same way I've always suspected the Novikovs of orchestrating my father's murder. But despite the accusations, Piotr and Vlad have remained allies.

"For blessed is Thy name, and glorified is Thy kingdom..."

I always suspected Kat believed the rumors, that she believed her uncles and cousins over her brothers, and that's why she left.

Could it be that she's finally seeing it Piotr's and Vlad's way?

She's a fighter, loyal to a fault. If she's here, it's because she's made a choice. Still, I can't shake the feeling that this is not what it seems.

For a moment, her eyes flicker up to meet mine, long enough for me to catch the fire still burning in them.

She doesn't look afraid; she doesn't look unsure.

She looks determined.

Her hand is warm in mine, soft against my calloused palm. She hasn't pulled away. I don't grip too tightly, but I don't let go either.

I slide the diamond ring onto her finger, watching as the fire in her eyes flickers. There's a moment of hesitation, a slight crack in the mask she's wearing.

When she looks at me, I feel it in an instant: a spark, a visceral connection, something neither of us can fake.

Her eyes widen just slightly. It's the smallest reaction, but I still see it, just like I see the other thing she's trying to hide —lust.

It's still there, just like it was six years ago; that same fire; that same hunger. I see it in the way her breath catches, the way her fingers tremble slightly as she slips the simple platinum band onto my finger.

She doesn't look at me again after that, but it doesn't matter.

I've seen enough.

She's still mine.

She always was.

CHAPTER 3

KAT

The reception is exactly what I expected—a display of wealth, power, and carefully crafted illusion.

They spared no expense. The chandeliers cast a golden glow over the room, glinting off crystal glassware and polished silver. The scent of expensive champagne and fresh floral arrangements lingers in the air, while the din of constant conversation hums in my ears.

Bratva politics disguised as a celebration. Everything about tonight is meant to send a message, a reminder to everyone in attendance of the bond between the Andreev and Fetisov families.

I can feel the stares, hear the whispers behind raised glasses, but neither holds my attention for long. Someone else already has it.

Pavel stands in the center of the room, commanding the space with his presence. Of course, he does; he's impossible to ignore. But it's to whom he's speaking that makes my stomach knot: Viktor Novikov.

Viktor is the leader of the Novikov Bratva, the man whose family is supposed to align with ours once Pavel is dead. The tension between them is obvious. I spot guards posted here and there, as if they're expecting a war to break out at any moment should the conversation take a turn for the worse. Pavel is calm and confident, sweeping his hand back and forth as he speaks.

Viktor's fingers twitch at his sides, his jaw tight. He's barely keeping it together. I wish I could hear what they're saying. Whatever it is, it's not sitting well with Viktor. Based on the sharp glint in Pavel's eyes, I can tell he's pressing him—backing him into a corner the way he does so effortlessly. Viktor looks like he'd rather be anywhere else.

The plan is simple: I kill Pavel, and in the confusion, the Novikovs step in. We ally, and when the dust clears from Pavel's assassination, my family will have solidified itself as the most powerful in the city. But seeing how Viktor's lip curls as he looks at Pavel with barely concealed contempt, I start to wonder how smooth this transition is going to be.

"Stop staring. You'll give yourself away."

Vlad's face is frustratingly neutral, but I know him well enough to see past the mask. There's the faintest trace of concern in his eyes. "You know, most women would spend their wedding reception celebrating, not skulking around trying to listen in on conversations."

"Please don't tell me I'm being that obvious."

"Only because I know you so well. Come have a dance with your brother. We need to act natural."

I don't argue. Instead, I let him take my hand and guide me onto the dance floor. The music swells around us as he leads me into a smooth waltz. We're moving in perfect rhythm, but, then his grip tightens slightly.

"You need to do better at playing it cool," he says.

I force a smile, tilting my head as if we're discussing something pleasant. "You don't think I'm acting cool?"

Vlad smirks, but there's no humor in it. "You're staring at him like you want him dead." His tone is pointed.

"I thought you said I wasn't being that obvious."

"Not yet, but you're awfully close. Hence, why I stepped in."

I scoff, shifting my gaze slightly. Pavel and Viktor are still locked in tense conversation. What the hell are they talking about? "Well, at least all eyes are off us for now," I say.

"It would appear that way."

"Which means we can discuss matters."

He sighs, frustrated. "What's on your mind?"

"As if you don't know." I subtly nod toward Pavel and Viktor. "I want to know what they're talking about."

Vlad doesn't glance their way. His disinterest is deliberate. "Does it matter?"

"Yes."

Vlad exhales, twirling me effortlessly before pulling me close again. "Viktor isn't important. The Novikovs will align with us, regardless."

I raise an eyebrow. "Not important?"

"They know what's good for them," Vlad says simply.

I huff. "So you think they'll just fall in line because we're so charming?"

Vlad's lip twitches slightly. "No, because they know what will happen if they don't."

"Are you saying they won't require a marriage?"

"They're not as strict as some of the more traditional Bratvas," Vlad says, his eyes flicking toward Pavel before shifting back to me. "They'll follow power when they see it. A marriage isn't necessary for that."

"You do realize our parents originally arranged this deal, right? Does that make them part of the strictly traditional Bratva?"

Vlad smirks as we turn. "Maybe, or maybe it was just their way of keeping us in line. After all, look at you now, Katerina Fetisova."

The name is like acid on my skin. My stomach twists, my jaw tenses. "Not for long."

Vlad's smirk fades. "Kat," he says, "you need to be careful. This plan is dangerous, and we both know Piotr doesn't give a damn about risk, as long as he gets what he wants."

His words sting, but I don't let it show. I can handle this. "I know what I'm doing," I reply, the knot in my chest tightening.

Vlad isn't convinced. "Maybe, but you can't control everything. If there's even a hint of doubt, you have to wait. Your safety is more important than Piotr's timing. Not everything needs to happen so soon. I'm not thrilled about the idea of my sister becoming a murderer."

I force my shoulders to relax, my face to remain neutral. "It's too late for that. This has been in motion for weeks. There's no turning back now."

"It's *not* too late," he says, his tone sharp. "Pavel is still alive. It's not too late until he's no longer breathing. You can still walk away from this."

"No, I want him out of the picture. I want our family safe and strong. I want—"

"Revenge."

Vlad's jaw locks; his teeth grind together. "Kat," he begins, "think about Ana. She needs her mother more than our family needs revenge."

My stomach drops. Ana. My daughter. The one person I can't think about right now.

I look away, anywhere but at him, my gaze sweeping over the ballroom. Guilt creeps into my core. The swirl of other elegant couples moving to the music does nothing to distract me.

Vlad is right. Ana is everything; the only thing that truly matters. But thinking about her now only makes this harder. "Ana is why I've survived this long. Ana is who I'm doing this for."

He lets out a mirthless laugh. "Really? She's the only reason you're doing this? It has nothing to do with your own needs?" He shakes his head. "I never should have agreed to this plan. As I've told you time and time again, I'm still not convinced Pavel's family is responsible for our parents' deaths."

"If you still think that, you're a fool," I shoot back.

"Things never added up for me."

"You're just worried."

"It's natural to fear the consequences of such a plan. When a man is murdered—especially a man like Pavel—it can set events into motion that we may not have anticipated."

My gaze snaps back to him, and I grip his hand tighter, my nails pressing lightly into his skin. "The deal is done, Vlad. Piotr is certain, and I trust him."

Vlad's eyes darken. "Do you? Do you really trust Piotr?"

The question hangs between us, thick and suffocating. I don't want to answer it, not tonight.

"I trust him enough," I concede, but the words are heavy, laced with bitterness. "He's my brother."

"And so am I."

Piotr is smart, ruthless. I've always known he plays the long game, manipulating every move with surgical precision. But that's what makes him a good leader. That's also what makes him a threat. I shake the thought away. It doesn't matter. "I'll do my part for our family," I say as I stare straight ahead over Vlad's shoulder. "Our parents' death will be avenged."

Vlad's expression is blank, but after a long moment, he nods reluctantly.

As if summoned, Piotr appears from among the crowd.

He stands at the edge of the dance floor, watching us with a polite smile that makes my stomach twist. It's practiced and smooth, but I know him too well to miss the calculation behind it.

"Mind if I cut in?" Piotr asks as he approaches.

Vlad looks between us, his reluctance apparent, but after a tense second, he nods and steps back.

"Go right ahead," he says as he gives Piotr my hand. "You know where I stand." He gives me a stern look before walking away.

I watch him leave, his movements stiff, shoulders tight. Guilt takes over again as an uneasiness settles in my gut.

Piotr firms up his grip on my hand. "What were you two talking about?" he asks in a light, casual tone. I know he's pressing me for information.

I meet his gaze, unflinching. "Vlad's worried about me."

Piotr's eyes narrow slightly. "Are *you* worried?"

I hold his stare, refusing to waver. "I'm nervous," I admit, because that much is true. I straighten my spine. "But I won't fail."

Piotr's smile widens, but it's not comforting—it's a warning. He leans in, his breath brushing my ear as he murmurs, "Remember your training, remember the plan. All you have to do is execute it."

The words send a chill down my spine, but I don't react. He pulls back, his expression softening. "I know what I need to do."

"The look on your face as you spoke to Vlad made me believe otherwise."

"You know, I don't appreciate your spying on me."

"That's part of my job," he says. "I wouldn't be a good boss if I didn't keep a close eye on things."

I turn my head to see Pavel coming toward us, his stride purposeful, his gaze locked solely on me.

Piotr catches the shift in my attention and turns slightly, his expression stoic, as my new husband stops in front of us.

"May I have the next dance?" Pavel asks, his voice smooth and deep, pulsing through my bloodstream like warm liquor. My breath catches in my chest, but I force my expression to remain calm.

"Of course," I reply.

Piotr's eyes linger on Pavel for half a second too long before he finally steps aside.

Pavel threads an arm around my waist and pulls me close; his body feels solid against mine. His body heat radiates through my silk dress.

I risk a glance up at him, the intensity of his gaze nearly undoes me.

"I'm glad you agreed to this," he says, his voice low in my ear. His thumb brushes the back of my hand; the lightest touch, but it wrecks me. "It's been a long time."

Six years, and damn him, my body remembers everything. The pull between us is instantaneous. The moment I took his hand at the altar, a familiar fire sparked to life with terrifying ease, a slow burn, dangerous and insidious.

CHAPTER 4

PAVEL

Fifteen minutes earlier...

Viktor Novikov stands across from me, swirling the vodka in his glass in slow, deliberate circles.

His expression is carefully fixed, his mouth slanted into something that almost resembles amusement, but I know better. The man in front of me isn't amused; he's calculating. He's testing the waters, searching for cracks, looking for any sign of weakness. He won't find any.

"Quite the spectacle, Pavel," he says in a smooth voice. "You always knew how to put on a show."

"This isn't a show," I retort. "This is my wedding."

He laughs. "Ah yes, that's right. And what better way to celebrate your nuptials than in top-notch style?"

"It goes beyond that. It's a necessary event for a necessary alliance."

Novikov hums, taking a sip. "Yes, an alliance. That's what we're calling it." His gaze flicks briefly to Piotr, who's laughing with a group of men near the bar, then to Kat, on the dance floor with Vlad. "I have to say, I didn't think she'd actually go through with it. It's been a long time since the lovely Katerina was in your life."

His words are deliberate and probing.

"I almost forgot that the Bratva families enjoy gossiping like schoolgirls as much as they enjoy their more lucrative businesses."

He chuckles. "Perhaps, but there's also the matter of precisely what is happening here tonight."

"A wedding—just what it looks like."

"With a wife who appears to be a million miles away? We know her heart isn't in this, but what about her head?"

I nod slowly. "She knows her duty."

Novikov chuckles again. "If you say so, though, I can't help but wonder what her thoughts will be after things play out. Does she know what's coming?"

I keep my expression neutral as he continues to fish for information. "She knows enough," I reply smoothly.

Novikov watches me for a long moment before sighing heavily. He leans forward, placing his glass on the table. "You and I both know this won't be as clean as you'd like it to be. The Andreevs are unpredictable. *Piotr* is unpredictable. I doubt he'll take kindly to being dictated to."

I finally allow myself to smirk. "Dictated to? No, that's not how I see it. It's a negotiation, Viktor. One where the terms have already been set. Whether Piotr is ready or not, the merger will happen within the week."

Novikov leans back, watching me with sharp, calculating eyes. He's not pleased, but he won't fight me on this, not yet. I drain the rest of my whiskey, then set the glass down.

"Enjoy the celebration," I tell him. "I'll see you at the next meeting."

Novikov picks up his glass again and raises it in mock salute. I make my way toward the dance floor. I've already dismissed the conversation. The real game will begin soon enough.

For now, my attention is on someone else: my wife.

I spot her immediately, dancing with Vlad. She's stunning, her ample curves hugged perfectly by the silk of her dress. Her hips are lush, and her breasts—*Christ*. I swallow hard, pushing back the rush of heat that threatens to take over my body. She's always been beautiful, but tonight, she's something else. Untouchable. A dream draped in white, looking every bit like the woman I once thought she'd be, the woman she now is.

Vlad says something to her, and she laughs, her full lips curving in a way that makes my cock twitch. That laugh causes memories to surface; how easily her laughter would arise when she was with me. My body tightens. It's been years, but my reaction to her hasn't changed. If anything, the hunger is more intense.

The song continues, and I head to the bar to refill my drink, taking the opportunity to watch them a little longer. She and Vlad are engaged in what looks like a lighthearted conversation, but I know better. The way Kat's eyes keep flicking around, she's searching for me in the crowd. It's obvious that I'm the topic of conversation, but what exactly is the context?

"Another of the same, Mr. Fetisov?" the bartender asks, an eyebrow arched in anticipation.

"Yes, please."

He refills my glass, and the song ends. Vlad and Kat continue to talk and dance, and it's becoming clearer by the second that the subject isn't mere congratulations and well-wishes. Then, Piotr emerges from the crowd. He heads toward them with purpose, he and his brother exchanging a few words. Vlad places Kat's hand in Piotr's, then walks away.

The bartender hands me my drink. I'm ready to join my wife. A little networking is expected at such an event, but after a while, it would look strange for the groom not to be with his bride at their wedding reception. I take a long sip, then set my glass on the bar before moving toward them.

Kat's eyes meet mine as I approach. Her spine stiffens as her fingers grip Piotr's shoulder. She recovers quickly, but her reaction to my presence is undeniable.

"May I have the next dance?" I ask. "And, if I haven't told you yet, you look like something out of a dream."

Her cheeks redden at the compliment. She looks away for a moment before turning those smokey eyes back to mine. She tilts her chin up. Clearly, she doesn't want me to see how much I affect her.

"Thank you."

I slide my arm around her waist, pulling her flush against me. Her breath catches, and it's the most satisfying sound I've heard all night. I lower my head slightly, inhaling the faint scent of her perfume—something sweet and familiar—and utterly intoxicating.

"Was the wedding to your liking?" I ask, my lips close to her ear. I can feel her body shiver.

She hesitates before answering. "It was lovely."

"Lovely." I chuckle, moving us into a slow, controlled rhythm. "I would have liked your input, but everything was so hastily arranged."

She lifts her eyes to mine, something guarded in her expression. "I'm sure it would have turned out the same, regardless."

There's that smile again—polite, distant. I fucking hate it.

I tighten my hold on her waist just slightly, just enough for her to feel the full press of my body against hers. "You weren't this shy when we were younger."

Her eyes flash. There she is.

"I've changed in the last six years," she says, her voice sharp, cool.

I smirk, lowering my head just a fraction. "In that case, I look forward to getting to know you again."

Her pupils dilate as she swallows hard. She's speechless. But then, she quickly recovers, her lips curling upward as she lifts an eyebrow. "How fortunate for me."

I bark out a laugh, a real one, throwing my head back as it rumbles from my chest.

"You know, no one has ever made me laugh like you do."

She blinks, then scoffs like she doesn't believe me. "That's ridiculous."

I shake my head. "No, it isn't." My fingers caress the small of her back, keeping her close. "I look forward to a lot more laughter with you, Kat."

Uncertainty, or perhaps confusion, clouds her expression for a moment. It's barely there, but I catch it. It's as if she doesn't know what to do. "We were something special once," I remind her. "We can be again."

Her breath hitches before I kiss her.

It's meant to be light, just a brief brush of lips, but the second we connect, that all changes. Her mouth parts slightly, just enough for me to deepen the kiss. She doesn't pull away. My grip tightens on her waist, and fuck, she's so soft and warm. Every inch of her fits against me, like we were made for each other, like she was made for me.

And for just a moment, I allow myself to believe she was.

CHAPTER 5

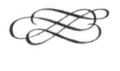

KAT

Pavel's lips leave mine, but the heat of the kiss lingers, sizzling low in my stomach.

I'm so turned on I can hardly think straight. My panties are soaked, and I want to squirm. I'm breathless, completely undone.

He lifts his hand, his fingers skimming my jaw before his thumb brushes the corner of my mouth, a slow, almost lazy, touch, like he's savoring the moment. He knows exactly what he's doing to me.

"So beautiful," he says.

The sound of a microphone crackling fills the space, followed by an announcement that sends my stomach plummeting. "Ladies and gentlemen, please raise your glasses to the happy couple!"

Pavel removes his arms from around my waist slowly, his fingers trailing along my back before he steps forward. He plucks two glasses of champagne from the tray of a passing waiter, effortlessly stepping into the role of the adoring husband.

He hands me a glass, then lifts his champagne flute, all eyes on him, on us. The room hushes into silence. Pavel glances down at me, snaking his arm around my waist again, before he speaks. "I wasn't planning on giving a speech tonight, but standing here now, looking at my wife..." He pauses, his gaze dragging over me like a physical caress, makes my skin heat up, "I've realized something."

I swallow hard in anticipation. The look in his eyes gives me anxiety.

"This marriage is supposed to be about family, about alliances, strength." He lets the words settle, his fingers tapping lightly against his glass. "That's how it is in our world. But for me, it goes beyond that."

The room is so quiet, you could hear a pin drop. Even Piotr is paying close attention, watching Pavel with a sharp glint in his eyes. Vlad is in the corner, a thoughtful expression playing across his features, as if he's trying to figure out what angle Pavel is playing.

Pavel shifts the flute so that the stem is between his two middle fingers, the glass resting in his palm. He turns it around in his hand as he continues, his other hand firmly pressed against my ribs. "Those who knew me years ago, knew Kat was my future. But then one day, she was gone." He exhales sharply, proof of the weight of his words. "That's life, is it not, always taking us in directions we don't expect."

My throat tightens as I try to guess where he's going with this.

"And here I am again, my life taking yet another direction. She's here, beside me. I don't believe in fate, but I do believe in second chances." His eyes flick to mine, his arm holding me close.

"This woman... She's fierce, she's smart, she's stubborn as hell."

A few chuckles ripple through the crowd, but I can't even break into a grin. I can barely breathe. "And after all these years, she's still the most beautiful thing I've ever seen."

I inhale sharply as the crowd gasps a collective, "Aww."

He turns back to the guests, lifting his glass slightly higher. "Everybody, please raise your glasses to my wife; to Kat Fetisova."

A chorus of, "To Kat!" rings through the room as the guests lift their glasses and drink.

I lift mine as well, my hand trembling slightly, as I take a sip of champagne. He's too good at this.

Pavel takes a long sip of bubbly before handing the microphone back to the DJ.

"What a speech," the DJ says, turning to address the crowd. "For us, the night is only getting started, but for the happy couple..."

Smiles appear on the faces of the guests. They know what the DJ is about to say.

"It's time for them to take their party of two upstairs!"

Bratva weddings are like medieval royalty—it needs to be announced that the couple is retreating to consummate the marriage.

Applause erupts, and a wave of cheers rolls through the crowd. The moment startles me, and I step back, trying to catch my breath. Pavel notices: He has a strange look on his face.

"Come," he says, taking my hand in his. "It's time to go."

I force a smile as I turn toward the guests, playing the perfect blushing bride, as we weave through the well-wishers.

It's suffocating—the hands reaching out to clasp ours, the shouts of congratulations, the envelopes stuffed with cash discreetly slipped into Pavel's grip. Bratva tradition—power disguised as generosity. Everyone in the room knows what this marriage means, what it cements, and they play their roles well.

As do I. I smile when I'm supposed to, nod when appropriate. I keep my hand tucked in Pavel's, trying to ignore the warmth of his grip, as I remind myself over and over of the plan.

Suddenly, Piotr is standing in front of me. His arms wrap me into a firm but brief embrace, his lips brush my ear as he whispers, "An extra vial of poison is in your makeup case. Add it to a glass of wine, and he'll be gone within the hour. You can do this, sister. Good luck."

I don't flinch; I don't react at all. Instead, I tilt my head slightly, as if he's murmuring something sentimental, some sort of brotherly advice.

Piotr pulls back, smiling down at me. I play the part of the devoted sister perfectly as I smile, pressing a soft kiss to his cheek. His hand tightens briefly at my waist before he releases me, shifting his focus to Pavel.

"Brother," he says simply, offering his hand.

I glance at Vlad, searching for reassurance. His gaze is serious and unreadable, but he finally steps forward and pulls me in for a hug. "Good luck," he says quickly and quietly.

I feel my chest tighten. "I don't need luck."

"Remember, it's not too late. It's never too late, until—"

Pavel reminds me it's time for us to head upstairs, preventing Vlad from finishing his sentence. He doesn't have to. I know I can back out until the second Pavel's lips touch the glass.

Vlad pulls back, his jaw twitching, but he says nothing else. Instead, he turns to Pavel, shaking his hand and giving him a subtle nod.

I inhale sharply as Pavel's hand settles on the small of my back, guiding me toward the exit. My skin burns under his touch, my body betraying me once again.

One more hour. That's all I have to get through.

The elevator doors slide shut, sealing me in with the one man around whom I should never let down my guard. My body still hums from his kiss and the way he made it feel like he still had the right.

I lean back against the wall, exhaling sharply. My feet are killing me. I bend down, ready to yank off my heels, but before I can, Pavel steps in front of me, his large hands wrapping around my wrists, stopping me mid-motion. His touch is firm, commanding.

"Let me," he says, already lowering himself to one knee.

I freeze. *Oh hell, no.*

Before I can argue, he slides his hands down my calves, taking his sweet time as he reaches my ankles. A sharp jolt of heat flares up my spine, and I grip the railing behind me for balance.

His fingers make quick work of the delicate straps, peeling them away from my skin with a gentleness that belies the dangerous man he's become. When his thumb brushes the arch of my foot, I have to prevent myself from moaning.

"You've been on your feet all night," he says. "You should've worn something more comfortable for the reception."

I narrow my eyes. "You mean like combat boots? Might not have had the same aesthetic appeal."

His lips quirk. "Maybe, but at least you wouldn't be wincing in pain."

His grip tightens slightly before he begins massaging my foot with slow, deep circles. My head tips back against the elevator wall, a sigh slipping out before I can stop it.

"Better?" he asks.

This man is ruining me with nothing but his hands, and he knows it. I swallow hard, trying to ignore the way my body reacts, trying to remind myself that I'm supposed to kill him tonight. But then he moves to the other foot, and I can barely suppress the full-body shudder that rolls through me. By the time he's done, I feel boneless, my body betraying me yet again.

He stands, my strappy heels dangling from his fingers as he towers over me. I reach for them, desperate for a reason to put some space between us.

"I've got them," he says smoothly, his tone making it clear that there's no point in arguing. "Let me help you."

I glare up at him, forcing my voice to remain cold and steady. "I don't need your help."

His smile is slow, almost indulgent. "You do; you just don't like admitting it. You've always been that way."

The doors slide open before I can snap back at him, and he gestures for me to step out first. The moment I do, my breath catches.

The view from our Four Seasons suite is breathtaking. Floor-to-ceiling windows overlook the New York skyline, the city lights glittering in the distance. A massive king-size bed sits in the center of the room, draped in luxurious white bedding. A bottle of champagne waits in an ice bucket on the table next to a tray of chocolate-covered strawberries. It's romantic, intimate.

Completely at odds with the fact that he will be dead before sunrise.

I take a step inside, my heart hammering against my ribs. I can feel Pavel's presence behind me like a dark shadow curling around my spine.

"You approve?" he asks.

"It's nice."

I hear him chuckle as I walk farther in, pretending to admire the view when, really, I just need to get my head on straight. I don't plan on sleeping with him tonight—or ever. But standing here, remembering how he felt, how he tasted, how easily he made me come all those years ago, my body has different ideas. I squeeze my eyes shut, willing the memories away.

Pavel was gentle that night, careful. He touched me like I was something precious, something he wanted to protect, to savor. I'd heard horror stories from other girls about how painful the first time could be, but he made it sweet and tender. I shake my head, pushing the thought away. No more thinking about the past.

Before anything happens, I need to freshen up, get out of this dress, get the poison.

End this.

As I turn, ready to excuse myself, Pavel is already there, holding out a glass of champagne. My breath catches as I stare up at him, his blue eyes burning into mine like he can hear my thoughts. Slowly, I take the glass, my fingers brushing his as I do. There's too much heat, too much history.

We sip in silence, the energy between us so thick it's nearly suffocating. I try to look away, to focus on anything else, but it's impossible. His gaze holds me, keeps me rooted in place, his presence swallowing me whole.

When I lower my glass from my lips, he takes it from my hand, setting it aside before stepping closer. I don't move. I don't even breathe. He kisses me, not like before, not teasing, not testing. This kiss is claiming.

And, at that moment, I know I don't have the strength to resist him.

CHAPTER 6

KAT

I should stop this now.

I'm here for one specific reason, and sex isn't it. But before I can even think, Pavel's hands are on me, his lips tracing a slow, devastating path down my neck, causing every rational thought to vanish in an instant.

"Tell me to stop," he says, as if sensing my inner turmoil.

I don't. I can't. "I... I..."

His mouth is at my collarbone, his fingers sliding over the delicate lace of my dress, teasing along the edge of the fabric like he has all the time in the world. He's not rushing; he's waiting. I hate that he still knows me so well. I tip my head back slightly, my breath uneven as his mouth ghosts over my skin. "Pavel..."

It's supposed to be a warning, but it comes out like a plea, like I'm begging him for more.

Perhaps I am.

His hands slide up my sides, fingers skimming my ribs, slow and controlled. He's holding back, giving me time to rebuff him.

"You're shaking," he says against my throat, his lips barely touching my skin. "Are you afraid of me?"

Yes.

But fear isn't what's making me tremble.

"Not afraid," I breathe, my voice barely above a whisper.

His lips curve against my skin, satisfied. "Good."

Then his mouth descends, his tongue tracing the hollow of my throat before he bites down, just hard enough to make me gasp. My hands fly to his shoulders, nails digging into the fabric of his suit, anchoring myself against the sheer force of him. He lifts his head, his gaze sharp, searching. "Last chance, Kat."

I hate him for giving me a choice. I grip the front of his shirt, twisting the fabric in my fists. "Don't stop."

His mouth crashes into mine, no hesitation, no restraint, just raw and consuming hunger. His hands slide down my back, cupping my ass as he pulls me against him. The hard length of his erection presses against my stomach through his slacks. I whimper as he groans into my mouth.

He lifts me up and carries me through the suite, never breaking the kiss. It's as if he owns me, like he always has. That thought should terrify me, but instead, it makes me ache.

He lowers me onto the bed, his body covering mine in an instant, pressing me into the soft mattress. The weight of him, the feel of him, the scent of him...it's all so intoxicating. My heart begins to beat faster, and I can feel my pulse everywhere.

His lips leave mine and begin moving down my throat; his breath is warm against my skin. He brushes his nose along my jaw, nipping at my earlobe before he whispers in my ear. "I've been thinking about this for six years."

I whimper again.

Fucking traitorous body.

He kisses down my chest as his hands slide up my thighs, pushing the fabric of my dress up slowly, torturously. I lift my hips, desperate for more, but he grips my thighs, holding me in place.

"So impatient," he murmurs, his fingers teasing the edge of my lace panties. "I remember how shy you were last time."

I feel my face flush. "Not anymore," I manage, my voice shaky.

He grins mischievously as he looks up at me. "No?"

His fingers slide beneath the lace, teasing over the already aching bundle of nerves at my center. I arch my back, a soft cry escaping me as his thumb moves in slow, lazy circles, just enough to make me desperate. "You are the same as I remember," he mutters. "So fucking soft. So fucking wet. So fucking perfect."

My breath stops as he hooks his fingers under my panties, pulling them down my legs. The air is cool against my heated skin, but it's nothing compared to the way his fingers feel trailing back up, teasing me, as he spreads my thighs open.

I gasp. My instinct is to close my legs, but he places his hand firmly on my thigh.

"No, Kat. Let me see you."

I obey, spreading my legs for him, allowing him to take in the sight of me. A smile spreads across his lips.

"You're so fucking sexy."

My body stills in anticipation, my breath coming in short, uneven pants.

He begins to stroke my most sensitive spot, teasing me with his touch, causing pleasure to surge throughout my body. His fingers slide through my slickness, parting me with ease, coating himself in the evidence of my arousal. I whimper, my head tipping back.

Pavel chuckles, his fingers lightly circling my clit again, just enough to make me shake. It's insane how he knows exactly how I need to be touched. "You're still so fucking gorgeous," he says. "You were made for me."

I bite my lip as memories rush in, and a moan escapes me when his fingers slide deeper before curling just right. I cry out, my hips lifting off the mattress.

"That's it, *krasivyy*, let me hear you."

His fingers move in perfect rhythm, stroking me from the inside as his thumb presses against my clit, working me until I'm panting and writhing, no longer able to think. I clench around him, my body tightening, my moans growing more desperate.

I'm so close. I can feel it building, spiraling, tightening in my core. And then, he stops.

I whimper in frustration, my body aching for release, but Pavel only smirks, dragging his wet fingers up my stomach and over my breast before gripping my chin, forcing me to look at him.

"You're so fucking wet for me, Kat."

My breath stutters as I squeeze my thighs together, desperate for friction.

"Tell me how much you want it."

My lips part, but nothing comes out.

His fingers tighten on my chin, demanding. "Say it."

I let out a shaky breath. "Please."

He hums in approval, his fingers slipping between my legs again, pressing deep, finding the spot that has me gasping. "Good girl."

Pleasure ripples through me, my back arching, my moan breaking into a cry as my pussy tightens around his fingers.

"You've been teasing me all night," he mumbles, dragging his lips down my stomach, his stubble scraping my sensitive skin. His fingers skate along the inside of my thighs, deliberately avoiding where I need him most.

"I think it's time I find out if you taste as good as you did back then."

I let out a sharp breath, my body already trembling, already wrecked from his words alone. He spreads my legs wider, his grip firm. I know I should tell him to stop, but I don't. "Pavel..."

He chuckles, a dark and amused sound. "I like it when you beg."

I let out a desperate whimper as his grip tightens.

"You like the way I touch you, don't you?" His voice is husky, his fingers dragging close, but not close enough.

I nod, my breath coming in small gasps now. He chuckles again, seemingly enjoying watching me squirm. I dig my fingers into the sheets, my hips lifting off the mattress once again. Pavel grins, his lips brushing my inner thigh before his mouth is fully on me.

His tongue slides through my slick heat, slow at first, teasing, deliberate. My hips twitch, a soft, helpless sound escaping me that I can't bite back. He groans against me as his tongue moves with purpose, with the full intention of wrecking me beyond repair. His hands grip my thighs, strong and unyielding, keeping me exactly where he wants me.

I gasp, my fingers fisting the sheets. "Oh. My. God."

Pavel hums against me, the vibration almost unbearable. My body bows off the bed, my thighs squeezing around his head, but he doesn't stop, he just keeps working me, lapping at me like he can't get enough. I'm squirming, panting, already teetering on the edge.

He groans, like he's enjoying this as much as I am. "You taste so fucking sweet," he mutters against me as his tongue flicks against my clit, devastating, circling, teasing. It's too much and not enough all at once.

"Pavel," I whimper, trying to grind against his mouth in order to chase the pleasure coiling tight in my belly.

"Stay still, baby."

He sucks on my clit, hard and purposeful, and I break.

The orgasm crashes over me like a tidal wave, violent and unstoppable, pleasure tearing through me so fast, so intense, I can't even think.

Pavel grins. He's not finished. Not even close.

His fingers slide into me, curling, hitting that magical place, pushing me toward the edge again. Before I can recover, before I can even breathe, I come again, crying out his name. He moves over me and presses his lips to mine. I can taste myself on them, can feel the smug, satisfied smirk as he kisses me.

I reach down and grip his cock, pressing its tip against my slick entrance. He enters me fully with one thrust, and I gasp, my nails digging into his back. Pavel groans, his head dropping against my shoulder.

"Fuck, Kat…"

He moves slowly, stretching me, filling me like he's claiming every part of me. My body clenches around him, still raw from the pleasure he's already given me, and he curses again. He thrusts into me hard, then slowly pulls back, repeating the motion as his mouth traces hot, open-mouthed kisses along my throat and down my collarbone. "Still so fucking tight."

My nails rake down his back, my body quivering beneath him.

"No one else has touched you, have they?"

I tense at the words. His head lifts, his blue eyes flashing, knowing. My heart slams against my ribs, but I can't lie. "No," I whisper.

His jaw twitches as something dark and primal flares in his gaze. The control he's been holding onto so tightly snaps, and suddenly, his mouth is on mine again, hot and devouring, all-consuming possession and raw hunger.

His hands are everywhere—gripping, claiming, branding. One fists my hair, yanking my head back, baring my throat to him as his teeth scrape along my skin. The other slides down, spreading my thighs wider, pinning me exactly where he wants me.

"You take me so fucking well," he growls against my lips, his voice nothing but gravel and sin. "Like you were made for me."

Indeed, I was. God help me, I was made for him.

He slams into me, deep and brutal, the force of it stealing the breath from my lungs. Every thrust is harder, faster, more punishing, and it's too much, too good, too perfect. My nails drag down his back, my hips arching up to match his rhythm. I'm desperate, ruined, so close I can practically feel myself unraveling.

The climax rips through me like lightning, my body clenching around him, my cry muffled against his shoulder as I bite down. The orgasm claims me, stronger than anything I've ever experienced before.

Pavel groans, a raw, guttural sound. He's right there with me, his body tensing, his rhythm faltering as he buries himself deep, filling me completely, his growl of release vibrating against my skin. His weight presses into me, solid and grounding, his breath hot against my neck. The scent of sex and sweat fills the room.

I should push him away. I should reach for the vial of poison.

But I don't.

I can't.

Because for the first time in six years, I don't feel empty.

CHAPTER 7

PAVEL

The wedding yesterday was nothing more than a spectacle, but what happened after was something else entirely.

Today we're on our way to Nassau in one of my private jets. The engines hum, cutting smoothly through the sky, but my focus isn't on the flight. My attention keeps shifting back to my wife.

Kat is curled up across from me, her body relaxed in sleep, her breathing deep and even. She's exhausted. It's not surprising, especially after how late we stayed up celebrating our nuptials.

I lean back in my seat, watching her, my lips curling in satisfaction. She's exactly as I remember: curvy and soft, made to be touched, taken, ruined. The silk slip dress she's wearing has ridden up just enough to give me a tease of her thigh. My jaw clenches. She still fits me like a glove.

Every minute of last night is still fresh in my mind. I knew she'd been uncertain at first. Her body was tense beneath mine, fingers digging into my shoulders like she wanted to shove me away—or claw me apart.

At least that's how it felt until the moment I slid inside her. Then her nails dragged down my back as she wrapped herself around me, making me feel like she'd never left. The memories flooded back. I couldn't believe it had been nearly a decade since we'd first made love.

"Relax, *krasivyy*," I whispered against her throat, dragging my hands slowly down the curve of her hip. "I've got you."

She nodded, but I knew she still wasn't sure if she was ready for what came next, so I took my time kissing her, tasting her, dragging my tongue down her bare skin, teasing her with my fingers, coaxing out every sweet sound she could make.

When I finally pushed inside her, filling her in one quick thrust, her head fell back and she gasped. I held still for a moment, allowing her to adjust, but when she rocked her hips up, I gave her everything.

Now, as I watch her sleep, my mind is still tangled with thoughts of her, the way she broke apart for me all over again.

I shake my head to clear the thoughts. I can't afford to get caught up in the memory of Kat's body. I'm on a short timeline and I need to focus. Four days is all I have, four days away from the power plays, the shifting alliances, the fucking knives pointed at my back.

Kat sleeps while I work, my laptop open, messages coming in, calls being made. The Bratva doesn't stop just because

I'm on my honeymoon. Upon our return, Piotr and I will be sitting at the same table, finalizing the merger of our two families.

The deal should be solid, but doubts keep creeping in, not just in my mind, but in the minds of my men as well. I remember what Nikolai, my number two, said, his arms crossed over his chest as he watched me with a cold, calculating stare.

"You shouldn't have agreed to this."

"It was necessary."

His jaw tightened. "Was it?"

I didn't answer.

"They sprung it on you too fast," he pressed. "I know you and Piotr have been close for a long time, but why all of a sudden is his sister ready to marry you after she ran away all those years ago? You know the rumors. The Andreev family blames you for what happened to Piotr's parents."

I shook my head. "Not Piotr or Vlad. They've remained loyal to me."

"Have they?" Nikolai asked. "Or have they just been biding their time until you let your guard down?"

I exhaled slowly, refusing to rise to his bait. "They want the same thing we do," I replied. "To take out the Novikov Bratva."

Nikolai had laughed bitterly, shaking his head. "It smells like a setup. We both know it."

I considered denying it, brushing it off. But I didn't, because a part of me knows Nikolai is right.

Nikolai's eyes had flickered with something similar to disappointment. "You're letting your history with them cloud your judgment."

I gritted my teeth. "I haven't let anything cloud my judgment."

He snorted. "Then why are we here? Why the hell did you agree to this marriage? To a deal that was practically dropped in your lap?" He paused then, his voice turning razor-sharp.

I stayed silent.

He shook his head, running a hand down his face. "Look, I get it. I do. You want to believe this is real. That it can all be as simple as merging our families and taking out the Novikovs together." His expression turned hard. "But I don't trust this, Pavel. And I sure as hell don't trust Piotr."

Suddenly, neither did I, not completely. But it's done. I'm married now, and on a plane with my wife to spend our honeymoon in Nassau.

I glance back at Kat, who shifts in her sleep, the slip dress riding higher, exposing more of her smooth, golden skin. I should be focused on staying alive, on securing my Bratva, my alliances, my power, but all I can think about is her lips on mine, her nails digging into my back, her body trembling beneath me as she screamed my name.

If this truly is revenge served cold, I don't know how I can resist it.

CHAPTER 8

KAT

The woman staring back at me in the mirror doesn't look like someone about to murder her husband.

I screwed up last night. Pavel should be dead by now, and Piotr is probably furious that he hasn't heard it's been done.

Soft curls frame my face, my makeup is flawless, and the silk slip dress, a gift from Pavel, handmade and chosen just for me, fits like a dream: thoughtful, elegant, far too intimate.

I'm in the magnificent bedroom of our hotel suite in Nassau. Seeing the ocean waves gently crashing onto the shore makes me realize it's been far too long since I've been to the beach.

I'd placed a quiet, discreet call to my little girl while Pavel was checking us in to the hotel. Hearing her voice was a balm to my soul. I've never been away from her this long, and I'm already itching to get back to her.

I step away from the window and reach for my purse, searching inside for my lipstick. My fingers brush against something small and cold.

I freeze. It's the vial.

I pull it from its hiding place in my makeup bag, holding it between my fingers, watching the dark liquid shift inside. So small, so unassuming, yet it holds the power to end all of this. A full dose in his drink, and by the time the night is over, so will he be. That's what I had agreed to do. But I didn't expect to want him again, *need* him again.

My stomach twists as memories from last night rush in, unbidden and unwanted: the way he touched me, the way he owned me, the way I let him.

I clench my fist around the vial, trying to drown out the memories from last night, but they persist—his mouth dragging over my throat, his hands gripping my hips, the raw, broken sounds I made as he pushed me over the edge again and again.

Pavel Fetisov is not just a man, he's a weapon, a force, a dangerous manipulator who takes what he wants. My parents are dead because of him. My loyalty belongs to Piotr, to our family, to my daughter, to vengeance.

Suddenly, a doubt creeps in, the small seed Vlad planted in my head last night at the reception. What if...? Piotr's conviction has never wavered. But conviction isn't the same as truth.

What if I'm about to kill a man for something he didn't do?

My hands begin to tremble. I could ask Pavel directly. Look him in the eye, demand the truth. Would he tell me? Would I believe him if he did?

A knock at the door shatters my thoughts, making me jump. I pull in a breath, shoving the vial back into its hiding place before smoothing my hands over my dress, hoping I can hide my anxiety.

"Kat?" His voice is low yet commanding. "Are you decent?"

I press the compact mirror back into place after smoothing on some lipstick, and swallow hard, forcing my tone to stay steady. "I am."

The moment Pavel steps inside, the air in the room changes; it physically shifts, indicating a force, a presence, a warning, has entered the atmosphere.

I turn to look at him and nearly choke. He's in a suit, tailored to perfection, the crisp white shirt open just enough to allow a sliver of tan skin to show. The black jacket hugs his broad shoulders, framing his powerful form, and his stance—calm, controlled, dominant—sends a curl of something traitorous low in my stomach.

His eyes darken the second they land on me, dragging over every inch with slow, deliberate appreciation. His lips press together, jaw ticking as he catches the deep neckline of the dress, the way it clings to my curves.

Heat pricks at my skin. I lift my chin in defiance, refusing to let him see how much he affects me. "Something wrong with the dress?" I ask, my voice sharp.

He steps closer, slow and measured. "You should wear red more often," he says, his tone smooth as whiskey, dangerous as a blade.

My throat tightens. "Red? This dress is emerald green."

He grins wickedly. "I'm not talking about the dress. I'm talking about your skin, the shade your cheeks turn when you come."

I stand my ground, forcing myself to meet his gaze. "You should stop staring," I reply coolly. "It's rude."

The grin fades momentarily before his lips curl up on one side, the smallest twitch of amusement. His fingers brush over my exposed collarbone, light as a whisper, the warmth of his touch setting fire to my skin. My breath catches as he leans in, his mouth grazing over the exact same spot, his lips warm and soft, his stubble rough.

A shiver rips through me. He kisses me, then again, making a slow, methodical trail along my throat, his hand sliding to the small of my back, anchoring me. My heart slams against my ribs.

"Pavel," I whisper, a warning without meaning.

He exhales; his breath hot against my skin. "Say it again. Say my name."

My stomach flips, heat flashing through me in a wave of need, anger, and confusion.

His lips find the other side of my collarbone, pressing into my skin, teasing, tasting. My arms wrap around his neck without thought, my fingers slipping into the short, dark strands at his nape, clinging to him because I simply can't fucking help it.

His hands slide down, pulling me closer, flush against his body. I can think of nothing else except how good he feels. My panties are soaked. God, why does he have this effect on me? How can I kill him when my body still belongs to him? His mouth claims mine, harsh and demanding, his tongue teasing past my lips before I can even think to resist.

He finally pulls back, his lips inches from mine, his breath hot against my swollen mouth, his blue eyes staring into my soul, burning, knowing. He sees the way I want him. The way I've always wanted him. His fingers lazily trail down my arm before he steps back, gaze locked on mine.

"Ready?" he asks.

I force a small, breathless laugh, masking the torment raging inside. "Ready," I reply.

I don't look back.

CHAPTER 9

KAT

Pavel's eyes burn into mine as we step out onto the private terrace of the restaurant, the sound of the waves crashing against the shore in the background. The setting is breathtaking: candles flickering on the table, a bottle of wine waiting to be poured, the moon casting a silver glow over everything. But it's not the ocean, the candles, or the wine that has my pulse pounding. It's him. His sharp suit, the way he moves like he owns every space he steps into, the heat in his gaze as he watches me.

"You should know," he says, "I nearly ripped that dress off you the second I saw you in it."

A thrill runs through me, my stomach flipping. "And why didn't you?"

His hand slides along my waist, his fingers brushing just enough to tease before he leans in, his breath warm against my ear. He pulls back, his eyes dragging over my body slowly, intentionally, possessively. "The only reason I didn't is because I promised you a beautiful evening."

Heat coils between my thighs.

I should be wary. I should be thinking about the vial hidden in my makeup case, the plan I was supposed to have executed already. Instead, I give him a sexy smirk. "I wouldn't have argued too much if we'd missed dinner," I admit.

His laughter is low and deep, wrapping around me like smoke. "Tempting," he says, his eyes flashing. "But when you taste this food, you'll be glad I tempered my urges."

~

He was right.

Dinner is delicious. The wine is rich, the food decadent, and the conversation easy. Flirting with Pavel feels natural, effortless, like we picked up right where we left off all those years ago. We talk about surface-level things, life, our families. I don't want him to get too close. I let him near my heart once, and it was the biggest mistake of my life. I cannot, *will* not, allow that again. I am, after all, intending to kill him.

His gaze lingers on me as he swirls his wine, his voice soft, curious, intentional. "Tell me something about you," he says, "something I don't already know."

I hesitate, looking out at the view. I can feel his eyes on me, studying, waiting. For a second, I consider giving him something real. A piece of myself. But then I remember what I came here to do. "Don't you know enough about me already?" I ask curtly.

"I could spend all night learning about you, Kat," he replies. "There's no such thing as enough."

I push my food around my plate. "There isn't anything else you need to know."

His jaw tightens, but he doesn't push. His brow furrows, as if a thought just occurred to him. "Let me send the guards away."

"The guards?" I look around, not spotting anyone in the restaurant who appears to be a guard.

"They're here, but they're very good at their jobs; that's why you don't see them," he says with a wink. "One second."

He sends a quick text. Next thing I know, three large men appear from different corners of the restaurant. One of them approaches our table, while the other two walk out the door.

He leans down next to Pavel and asks, "Are you sure? I'm not entirely convinced this place is secure."

"I'm sure. Stick around but stay back."

"Yes, Boss."

With that, he, too, vanishes into the crowd before exiting out the side door.

"How's that?" he asks.

"Dangerous and risky. You should listen to your men. There are plenty of people who might want one of us—or both of us—dead."

I arch an eyebrow as Pavel stands, offering me his hand.

"A walk?" he asks.

I slide my palm into his, and the second his fingers wrap around mine, sparks seem to fly invisibly around us. I should pull away.

But I don't.

~

The sand is cool beneath my bare feet, the waves rolling in, steady and hypnotic, the scent of salt clinging to the breeze. The hem of my dress flutters around my ankles, teasing against my skin. It should be a perfect night.

"We can be happy together, you know," he says. He hasn't let go of my hand all night.

I'm about to respond when music begins to spill from a club nearby—a rhythmic pulse, low and sultry—vibrating through the air. Without warning, Pavel spins me, then pulls me against him, his arms locking around my waist in one fluid movement. I gasp, laughing before I can stop myself. "What are you doing?"

Pavel smirks, his blue eyes flashing. "Dancing with my wife."

"This isn't a dance floor," I point out, though my arms betray me as they slide up his chest, my fingers curling into his shirt.

His grip tightens on my waist, his lips brushing the shell of my ear as he sways us to the music. "It is if I say it is."

Cocky bastard.

I roll my eyes, but I don't fight it. I tell myself it doesn't mean anything. The heat between us, the way he looks at me, the way he touches me... It's nothing more than my body's natural response to the history between us.

Lust. Nothing else.

But when he dips me back, his strong arm holding me like a promise, his mouth brushing mine in the barest tease of a kiss, it doesn't feel like nothing. It feels like everything. We move together, our bodies pressed tightly together, our steps effortless. Pavel has changed. He's still dangerous, still powerful, but there's something different about him now. He's calmer, more at ease. He took over the Bratva at a very young age. I remember how serious he was back then, always strategizing, planning, watching. But tonight he's just a man dancing with his wife.

And for one reckless, fleeting second, I let myself be his wife.

Suddenly, three men stumble out of the club. One of them whistles, his eyes crawling over me.

"Damn, look at that ass," he says, laughing.

I freeze.

I haven't been called out for my body in years. I've learned to love my curves, to own them, to embrace the power in the way I command space. But the way he said it felt like an insult, causing a sharp and unexpected sting.

I feel Pavel stiffen, his grip on me tightening as he slowly turns toward the man.

Oh, no.

"Walk away," I whisper, pressing a hand against his chest. "He's not worth it."

His jaw works back and forth, his eyes fixed on all three men. I have no doubt that he's fantasizing about taking them apart with his bare hands.

"Pavel. Please. Let it go."

He nods once, takes my hand, and begins to lead me away.

The guy laughs louder before yelling out, "Where you goin', chubby chaser?"

Pavel turns around, slow and controlled, then tilts his head. His fingers flex at his sides as he steps into the guy's space, forcing him to take a step back. "You think that was funny?" Pavel asks in a low yet lethal tone.

The guy scoffs, but his bravado is cracking under the weight of Pavel's stare. "What? I can't compliment your taste? Some of us like our women a little—"

He doesn't get the chance to finish, as Pavel's fist connects with his jaw so hard, so fast, I can hear the impact over the music from the club. The guy's head snaps back, his body landing in the sand with a heavy thud. He groans, blood dripping from his nose. One of his friends takes a step forward, fists clenched.

"You want to join him?" Pavel asks.

The man hesitates before glancing down at his friend, still lying in the sand clutching his nose, choking on his own blood. He looks back at Pavel and backs down, muttering something under his breath as he grabs his groaning friend, hauling him up. The third guy remains silent as he takes one last look at Pavel. Noting the raw violence simmering just beneath the surface, he makes a smart decision: He turns and bolts.

Pavel's hand finds mine again, his grip firm as his thumb brushes over my skin, making me feel safe and protected. His voice is calm and unbothered as he says, "Let's go."

We walk away in silence, my heart pounding, not because I'm scared, but because I've never felt more wanted and cherished in my life.

CHAPTER 10

KAT

One hand is laced with mine, the other skimming the curve of my waist as we walk. Every few steps, his fingers trail lower, brushing over my hips, squeezing my ass like he's claiming me.

"I happen to love your body. Every inch of it."

A shiver races down my spine. I should be used to this by now—the way he strips me bare just with his voice, the way he worships me without hesitation, never apologizing for wanting me. He's still a killer. Still the *pakhan* of one of the most powerful Bratvas. Still a man capable of terrible, brutal things. But did he truly murder my parents? Could the man who just defended my honor so effortlessly have taken everything from me?

Doubt creeps in, a whisper I can't ignore. It's unshakable. I never was a hundred percent certain about Pavel's guilt. I'd let Piotr's conviction become my own, even though Piotr never produced any actual proof. What if he's wrong? What if I'm about to destroy a man who isn't my enemy after all?

I need to know the truth.

The vial in my makeup case will stay put for now.

∼

The moment we step onto the terrace of our suite, I know I'm in trouble. Pavel's grip tightens around my hand. He hasn't let go of me since we left the club, and the air feels charged with the adrenaline from the earlier confrontation.

I barely have time to react before he spins me and presses me against the railing, his body caging me in. I pull in a sharp breath, my pulse pounding.

"Pavel—" His lips are on mine before I can continue.

The kiss is raw and punishing, heated and demanding, rough and possessive. I don't fight it. I don't push him away. I kiss him back with equal fervor. His hands are everywhere before reaching up into my hair, tilting my head back so he can kiss me even more deeply. "I've wanted to rip this damn dress off of you all night."

His words make my knees go weak before I feel my dress being lifted up my thighs, baring my skin to the night air. I shiver, but not from the cold. His fingers run over my body, rough and deliberate. I inhale deeply, then let it out slowly, my head falling back against the railing, my fingers gripping his shirt.

"Fuck, Kat," he says, his breath hot against my lips. "You're already soaked."

I moan, rolling my hips into his touch. Pavel strokes me, teasing me, pushing me closer to the edge with every slow, deliberate movement.

"This is what you want, isn't it?" His fingers work harder, faster. "To be seen? To be fucked out here where anyone could be watching as I make you come?"

A whimper escapes me. I don't know whether it's the words or the way he's touching me, but my body is on fire, spiraling, losing control.

His free hand slides up, curls around my throat, and tilts my chin up, forcing me to look at him.

"Let me see it," he growls. "Let me see you come."

The pleasure tears through me, my body trembling, my moan breaking against his lips as he kisses me through it. His fingers don't stop until I'm spent, breathless, and trembling.

Finally, he pulls away. I'm still panting, my pulse a frantic drumbeat in my chest when he lifts his hand to his mouth. I watch, dazed and helpless, as he sucks his fingers clean, his eyes locked onto mine.

Fuck.

I barely have time to catch my breath before he grips my thighs and lifts me up. I automatically wrap my legs around his waist, my hands fisting into his shirt.

"I'm not done with you, Kat," he says, walking us back into the suite.

"Not even fucking close."

CHAPTER 11

PAVEL

I hold Kat with one hand under her ass while I close the glass door to the suite. Once inside, I don't hesitate. I don't set her down gently. I push her up against the wall, my mouth at her throat, dragging my teeth over her pulse, feeling it race.

Her dress is bunched up around her hips, her breath sharp and uneven, her fingers clutching at my shoulders. I fucking love the way she holds onto me. "You like putting on a show for me, don't you?" I growl against her skin, my teeth grazing her collarbone. "You like knowing anyone could have seen you come for me."

She gasps but doesn't answer. I release her legs slowly, then smack her ass, firm but light, just enough to make her jolt. Her head snaps up, eyes wide, lips parting on a breathy moan. I can't help but smirk. Her throat works as she swallows. Then, so quiet I almost don't hear it, she says, "Yes."

Fucking perfect.

I drag the dress over her head, savoring the way it slides off her skin, letting the fabric slip through my fingers as it falls to the floor. She's bare. Beautiful. Mine. I take my time looking at her. Thick, perfect curves—the kind that beg to be touched, claimed, worshiped. Soft thighs, a full, round ass that feels like heaven in my hands. "You have no idea how fucking gorgeous you are, do you?"

Her cheeks flush, her lips parting like she wants to argue, like she wants to tell me I'm wrong, but I won't let her. My hands skim her body over her full, heavy breasts, my thumbs dragging over her nipples, watching the way they harden under my touch.

A deep growl rumbles in my chest. I want her like this all the time—breathless, flushed, desperate. My hands wander lower, gripping her hips, relishing the way they curve perfectly beneath my fingers. Every soft, thick inch of her drives me insane. She's all mine, and she is perfect.

She's watching me with those dark, smoldering eyes, her chest rising and falling in uneven breaths, waiting. I'm going to make her wait even longer.

I pick her up again and carry her to the bed. Laying her down gently, I run my palms up and down her body, slow and deliberate, teasing the shape of her waist, the curve of her hips. She arches into my touch, impatient, her fingers clutching the sheets. My thumb skims the inside of her thigh, though not quite where she needs me, and she whimpers.

Good. I want her desperate.

"You were dripping for me outside," I mutter, relishing the way her body shudders beneath my touch. "Let's see if you still are."

She bites her lip, her hips thrusting upward in a silent, breathless plea.

I unbutton my shirt slowly as she watches, my eyes telling her exactly how much I want her. Her gaze tracks every movement. I slide my belt loose, then hold it in my hands, tilting my head slightly. Her eyes widen in anticipation as she looks at the leather strap. "Do you want me?"

Her gaze snaps back to mine, heat flashing behind it. "Yes."

I move closer, fisting a hand in her hair, tilting her chin up. "Then show me."

She licks her lips, then slides off the bed. "Come here," she says, indicating for me to sit on the edge. She gets on her knees in front of me.

Fucking hell.

My jaw tightens as she reaches for my waistband, her fingers trembling slightly as she pulls my zipper down, her fingers brushing against me, making my cock twitch in response. She slowly pulls my slacks down, her eyes never leaving mine. She kisses along my legs as she works her way up, then without hesitation, her lips wrap around me.

A groan rumbles deep in my chest, my head dropping back.

Her tongue swirls around the head of my cock, teasing, dragging slow, wet circles before she takes me deeper, her lips stretching around me. She's eager, her fingers stroking me with purpose, her other hand gripping my thigh. Her movements are controlled, precise.

Fucking hell, the way she looks up at me with those dark, knowing eyes, locking onto mine as she takes me even deeper. She knows exactly what she's doing to me. She hums around me, the vibration shooting straight to my core. My fingers tighten in her hair, gripping the soft strands, guiding her pace.

Slow. Savoring.

I move her faster, making her take more, her lips stretching even wider, her soft moan vibrating through me like a goddamn earthquake. I grit my teeth, my jaw clenched so fucking tight it aches. Heat licks up my spine, my muscles locking. "Fuck, that's it."

She moans again, that filthy, desperate sound muffled around my cock, sending another sharp jolt of pleasure through me. She's too perfect. Too willing. Too fucking good.

And it's wrecking me.

I know I won't last much longer. I pull her away before I lose every ounce of control, dragging her up onto the bed, then climbing on top of her. She gasps, arching into me, her hands reaching. I grab her wrists and pin them above her head. "Not yet."

I trail my mouth lower, every soft sound she makes, every tremor of her body only making me hungrier.

When I finally hook her legs over my shoulders, she barely has time to react before I bury my tongue in her. She cries out as her hands fly to my hair, fingers twisting, pulling. I smirk against her, dragging my tongue through her slick heat, slow, savoring, teasing her with featherlight strokes.

Her moans are breathless and desperate, her body shifting, trying to take more. I grip her hips tight, holding her still. She whimpers, her back arching off the bed. I circle my tongue over her clit, slow and devastating, then flick harder, faster, setting a rhythm that has her writhing beneath me.

I'm in no hurry. I want her to feel this, to enjoy it. I suck hard at her clit, teasing her with my tongue, feeling her thighs trembling around my shoulders. She's so close, her legs tightening, her breathing ragged. "You taste fucking delicious," I mutter, lapping at her just right, drawing her higher, keeping her at the edge.

She gasps, then curses my name before she falls apart, body shaking, legs clenching around me as she comes, hard and fast. Her pleasure rolls through her in waves as I stroke her through it, not stopping until she's completely sated.

I press a final kiss to her inner thigh, grinning against her soft skin. Then I move up her body, ready to ruin her all over again. I flip her onto her stomach, my hand sliding up her spine, then back down again as I drag her hips up, positioning her exactly how I want her. She shivers in anticipation, need, surrender.

"Hands on the headboard," I order.

She hesitates just for a second. Then, with a soft whimper, she obeys, gripping the carved wood, bracing herself.

Good girl.

My palm trails over the curve of her ass, smoothing over the soft skin before I give it a sharp smack. She gasps in surprise, but she doesn't move away.

"You like that, don't you?"

I can see her fingers tightening on the headboard. "Yes, sir," she whispers.

Fuck. The way she says it, breathless and obedient, with just a hint of defiance underneath...

A low growl escapes my throat, and I grip her hips, lining myself up, teasing her with the head of my cock. I slide in just a little, then pull out. She pushes back, desperate, a frustrated moan spilling from her lips. I continue the movement, tormenting her, making her squirm, making her beg. "Tell me how much you want it."

She presses her forehead to the pillow. "I need it. Please."

I sink in, slow and deep, stretching her, filling her inch by inch. She groans as she arches her back, her fingers curling tighter around the headboard. "You take me so well," I say, dragging my hands over her back, her hips, holding her still as I thrust deeper.

She gasps, pressing back against me. I grip her hips tighter, keeping her right where I want her.

I set the pace—slow, deep, deliberate. Her breathing turns erratic, every thrust pushing her higher. Her body clenches around me, her moans turning to desperate cries. She's helpless, and she's close.

I reach around, fingers finding her clit, stroking until she lets go. She cries out my name, her body convulsing around me, dragging me dangerously close to the edge. But I'm not finished yet. I flip her onto her back, pressing her into the mattress before she can even catch her breath.

Her eyes are hazy, dazed, lips parted as she looks up at me. Her legs instinctively wrap around my waist, locking me in place, pulling me in deeper. I groan, thrusting harder, faster, chasing that final, devastating high. "I want to see your face when you come this time," I growl, my forehead pressing against hers.

Her hands claw at my back, her nails raking over my skin.

"You're mine, Kat," I whisper, our lips brushing.

Her fingers tangle in my hair as she presses her lips against mine.

I kiss her back—hot, deep, punishing—as I thrust into her one last time, pushing her over the edge, her moans swallowed by my mouth as she comes again. The sensation drags me under with her, a guttural sound tearing from my throat as I spill inside her, losing myself completely. I collapse on top of her. Neither of us moves for a long time.

Her body is still trembling beneath me, her breath coming in soft, uneven gasps. I'm still inside her, my weight braced on my forearms, my breath heavy against her skin. After a couple of minutes, I roll to the side. She curls into me, pressing her face against my chest.

I inhale sharply, surprised by the sudden, unexpected softness of it. She shifts; her voice barely audible. "Stay."

One word. A quiet plea.

I don't answer. I don't move.

I stay.

CHAPTER 12

PAVEL

The ocean stretches out endlessly, glittering like a sheet of diamonds. The air is thick with the scent of sea salt. A few yards away, our private chef prepares a delicious meal of fresh, grilled seafood.

Kat isn't a woman who gets lost in thought for no reason. She looks calm, relaxed even, but I know better. She's here physically, but she's somewhere else entirely mentally. Something seems off. I think back to last night, replaying our lovemaking. I'd taken her, claimed her, made her mine. For a woman like Kat, who's bold and independent, that dynamic does not come naturally.

But she took me willingly, wholeheartedly, and it was amazing. Maybe she's having regrets about marrying me, but I sure as hell don't.

She pushes a piece of fruit around her plate, her gaze locked on the horizon, but there's no focus behind it.

I pick up my wineglass and take a slow sip, watching her carefully, giving her time to pull back from wherever her mind has taken her. But she remains locked in drifting further away.

I set my glass down. "What are you thinking ab

Her fork stills, her fingers tightening around it just slightly.

For a brief second, her expression appears unguarded, then just as quickly, the blank stare returns. She tucks a loose strand of hair behind her ear, blinks once, and pastes on a practiced smile. "I was just wondering what your house looks like," she replies, reaching for her wine lass.

Complete lie. Too easy. Too polished.

I don't call her out on it. Not yet anyway.

"My house?"

She nods.

"Yeah. I mean, we're husband and wife now. That means we're going to be living together. I'd like to know what kind of home I'm moving into."

Kat has never been good at lying, and in this moment, she's lying through her teeth. I know every little tell she has, even after being apart all this time. The slight hesitation before she speaks, like she's filtering her thoughts. The barely-there shift in her posture, like she's bracing for something. The way her fingers tap against the table in a calculated beat as she prepares her next move. I know her too well. In my line of work, a man lives or dies by how well he can read people.

I lean forward, resting my forearms on the table. "It's a penthouse. Takes up the entire top floor of the building."

Kat tilts her head, considering. "Do you own the whole building?"

"I do."

Her lips part just slightly, and I can see the wheels turning in her head, the way she's processing this little piece of information.

"It's in Tribeca," I continue. "The building is on a quiet street, tucked between old industrial lofts that have been turned into multimillion-dollar condos. A lot of old money, but also a lot of new money trying to prove itself. I don't deal with any of that."

I grin, taking another sip of wine. "There are a few tenants on the lower-level floors, but I rarely see them. I have a private elevator that goes up to my penthouse."

Kat sets her glass down, her fingers running idly over the rim. "I think I remember it," she says, more to herself than to me. "When we were younger, I begged Piotr to take me with him to pick you up once."

I nod. "You were maybe sixteen?"

"Something like that. I didn't go inside, though. Piotr made me stay in the car."

Of course, he did. Even back then, Piotr had a tight grip on what she did, where she went, whom she spoke to.

I stretch my legs out beneath the table, noticing the way she tucks her hair behind her ear again—another tell. She's working through something in her mind.

"My father owned the building back then," I tell her. "It was one of the first major properties he acquired in the city.

At the time, our fathers had plans to merge our families; a full alliance. They were going to move your family into one of the lower floors once everything was in place."

Kat stiffens, tension creeping into her shoulders. I pause, watching her, assuming the reaction is from grief. I exhale sharply.

"I shouldn't have brought that up. I know it's a painful subject."

I expect her to say something. To brush it off or nod in agreement. But before she can respond, one of my bodyguards steps forward, his voice low as he whispers into my ear. The air shifts before I even hear the words.

"Novikov made a move."

The information lands like a gunshot.

I don't react immediately. I finish my last sip of wine, set the glass down, and exhale through my nose before speaking. "What kind of move?"

"A power play. Direct challenge."

My jaw tightens, but my expression remains stoic. I knew it was coming. I fucking knew it. Novikov has been waiting for an opening, and I gave him one the second I stepped away. The second I let my guard down.

Kat is watching me, eyes sharp, calculating. Her phone rings. We both glance at the screen.

Piotr.

Kat reacts quickly, putting the call on speaker before answering. "You're on speaker," she announces immediately, "and Pavel's here with me."

There's a beat of silence, then Piotr's voice fills the air. His hesitation before speaking gives me the impression that he had something else he wanted to discuss with his sister, something he didn't want me to hear.

"Speak, Piotr. What's going on?"

"Novikov's men hit multiple businesses last night," Piotr says. "Locations that were under both Andreev and Fetisov protection."

"Go on," I say.

"A homemade bomb went off at one place, drive-by shootings at the others. And before you ask, no visuals on the shooters. Cars were found a few hours later, stripped down to nothing."

I don't move. I don't blink.

"How bad is the damage?" I ask, my voice like ice.

"Four dead," he says.

Kat stiffens beside me.

"All civilians," Piotr continues. "Innocents. Several more injured. The businesses are destroyed."

A muscle ticks in my jaw as rage coils inside me, but I don't let it show. Novikov wants a reaction. He wants me reckless. I won't give him that.

Kat shakes her head, her fingers tightening around the stem of her wine glass. Her horror is written all over her face.

Novikov made a sloppy, desperate play, and now innocent blood has been spilled.

Unacceptable.

I let the silence stretch, let the weight of the moment settle before I speak. "Kat and I will be leaving for New York within the hour."

Piotr doesn't sound surprised. "Good."

I end the call without another word.

Kat exhales slowly, placing her hands in her lap. She doesn't look at me, and for a moment, neither of us speaks. Finally, I stand. She lifts her chin, meeting my eyes.

"I'm sorry," I tell her. "I have calls to make."

"I'll handle the bags," she says simply.

I step toward her, reaching out before I can second-guess myself. My hand cups the back of her head, my fingers threading through her hair as I press a slow, deliberate kiss to her forehead. Her breath hitches. I step away and reach for my phone.

I have a war to handle.

CHAPTER 13

KAT

I watch Pavel disappear into the suite with his phone already pressed to his ear. His expression is hard, cold. He moves with purpose, his broad shoulders squared, his entire presence shifting into complete focus. I swallow, turning to the bodyguard stationed near me. He's quiet, yet watchful.

"I'm going to my room," I tell him, smoothing the front of my dress as I stand. "I'm going to pack. I'll let you know when I need my bags taken to the car."

He nods once. Nothing more. No further reaction, no questions. Just obedience.

I grab my phone and head straight to the bedroom, closing the door behind me, exhaling sharply. My hands curl into fists as I press them against the cool surface of the door, my pulse and my mind both racing. Something doesn't feel right.

I call Vlad. He picks up on the second ring.

"What the hell is going on?" I demand.

Vlad sighs on the other end of the line. "You already know."

"Novikov's men attacked businesses under our protection," I say, pacing the length of the room. "Four innocent people are dead. That's what I know." I stop at the edge of the bed, my fingers curling into fists again. "But that's not all of it, is it?"

Vlad hesitates. He's deciding what to tell me and what to keep to himself. My stomach knots. "Vlad. Don't you even think about keeping me in the dark. Is Ana safe?"

"Of course," he replies instantly. "You know I would never let anything happen to her."

"Then what is it you're not telling me?"

"Piotr knew about the attacks fast." He pauses. "Too fast."

A chill skates down my spine. "What are you saying?"

"Nothing," Vlad snaps, but there's tension in his voice. "I shouldn't even be telling you this."

I clench my jaw. "Vlad, don't do that. Don't say something like that, then act like it's nothing."

Silence.

I sit down and grip the edge of the bed, my nails digging into the fabric. "Tell me what you're thinking."

"There's nothing to tell."

"Vlad—"

"No. That's it. End of discussion."

I sigh heavily, frustration coursing through me. But I know when Vlad shuts down a conversation like that, he's not going to open it again. At least not right now.

"You and Pavel are leaving soon?" Vlad asks.

"Yes. Not sure when exactly, but I know Pavel wants to be out of here within the next few hours."

"Alright. Stay safe. Keep me in the loop about everything, and I mean *everything*. We need to execute this plan sooner than later. Emphasis on sooner."

Something in his tone makes my throat tighten. It's almost like he's warning me. Maybe I'm just being paranoid. Vlad is the brother I can trust. So does that mean there's a brother I *can't* trust? The thought is like a punch to the gut.

"I will. You won't be left in the dark."

As soon as the words leave my mouth, I doubt their sincerity. I'm only telling him what he wants to hear.

Just as I'm about to end the conversation, wanting to get away from it before it makes me think too much, Vlad speaks again.

"Kat."

"Yeah?"

"Piotr wants to talk to you. Stay safe, sister."

"You too." My pulse pounds in my ears, drowning out the sound of the ocean just outside the window. I should have known this was coming.

I hang up, and the phone immediately rings. I answer the call without saying a word. Piotr's voice comes across the line, cold and cutting.

"Why is your husband still alive?"

I close my eyes for a second, take a deep breath, and force my voice to remain steady. Calm. Controlled.

"There are bodyguards with us at all times. I haven't had the chance to slip it into his drink or food with all those eyes on us."

It's a weak excuse, and I know it. He knows it.

"This never should have gone this far," he says, anger edging his tone. "He was supposed to die on your wedding night."

"Well, it didn't happen that way. And considering I'm the one doing the deed, you could give me a little leeway."

He chuckles. "Sister, if only you knew the things I've done to keep this family safe and secure, things way more malicious than slipping a little poison into a cocktail."

I suppose he has a point there.

"I'm waiting for the right moment, Piotr. Pavel rarely lets me out of his sight, and I've already mentioned the bodyguards."

Silence stretches for half a beat before his response slams into me like a whip crack. "Are you fucking him?"

I freeze. My pulse roars in my ears as fury surges through me, white-hot and immediate. "Don't talk to me like that," I snap, my voice sharp, biting.

He doesn't acknowledge my response. His voice only grows colder, sharper, and more ruthless. "Then do your duty. Kill that bastard."

I clench my jaw so hard, my teeth ache. My fingers dig into my palm, nails pressing into flesh as I grip the phone, my rage barely contained. I feel nothing but hatred toward him at this moment.

"Jesus fucking Christ, Katerina. Don't tell me you've fallen for him again."

I exhale slowly, trying to maintain my fury before responding. "My feelings for him ended when our parents died."

Obviously, that's a lie.

Piotr doesn't say anything for a moment. He just lets the silence stretch, his cold presence reaching me through the phone.

He delivers his final words, clipped and cold before the line clicks off. "Remember where your loyalty should lie."

I stare at my phone, my breath coming in sharp, uneven bursts, my grip so tight I think I might snap the damn thing in half. This isn't how our father taught them to lead. Our father commanded respect, but he didn't rule through cruelty. He didn't belittle. He didn't manipulate the people closest to him, treating them like pieces on a chessboard. He didn't need to, because people followed him willingly because they believed in him; because they respected him. Piotr demands loyalty, but he gets it through fear.

I rub a hand over my face. Why couldn't I have done what I was supposed to do? My heart already knows the answer. It's because, for the first time in years, I feel something. I've enjoyed the time I've recently shared with Pavel. I fell in love with him once before, and he's the father of my child—even if he doesn't know it.

My throat tightens and I press my lips together, blinking against the sudden sting in my eyes.

Damn it. Vlad was right.

This plan was never going to work. Killing Pavel was never going to be easy, but now it seems impossible. I feel stuck between my familial loyalty to Piotr, who expects me to commit murder, and Pavel, who has done nothing but make me feel seen, desired, and, God help me, cared for in the last two days.

I don't want to kill him. I don't want anyone else to kill him either. But if his family really was behind the murder of my parents...

I groan, frustration building in my chest. I reach for the suitcase, flipping it open with a little too much force, and start throwing things in, my movements careless and erratic. My hands shake as I clumsily fold a dress, smoothing it out, trying to focus on the motion. I can't let Piotr get to me. I can't let him be the one who decides my future.

But I also can't ignore the truth. Pavel is dangerous. He has blood on his hands. He lives a life of violence and power. But is he really guilty of murdering my parents? Or is Piotr just using me the same way he uses everyone else?

The thoughts make me feel sick, because if that's true, and my own brother has been manipulating me into doing his dirty work, into carrying out his brand of vengeance for his own motives, I've wasted six years hating the wrong person.

CHAPTER 14

KAT

Two weeks later...

Pavel has been a ghost since we returned from our honeymoon. He leaves early, returns late, and when he's home, his mind is elsewhere. Once a day, he'll offer a brief form of affection—always a fleeting moment in passing—before he's out the door or vanishing into his office for hours on end, busy with meetings and phone calls.

It's as if he's performing the bare minimum in order to be considered an attentive husband, playing a role, and nothing more. There are no late-night touches. No whispered desires. No heated hands exploring my body, making me squirm as he buries his cock inside me.

I hate how much I miss it; how much I miss *him*.

I glance around the penthouse, trying to shake the thoughts away, but they cling to me like a shadow. His home is beautiful. A modern penthouse in Tribeca, with glass walls that frame the Manhattan skyline. Each room is tastefully decorated, furnished with sleek, modern furniture, expensive art on the walls, and plush rugs, straight from the pages of the latest design magazines.

It's too perfect, too controlled. Too empty.

Everything is clean and precise, the reflection of a man who doesn't like anything out of place. There are no personal touches. No family photos. No warmth. I imagine the only rooms he really spends any time in are his office and his bedroom.

It doesn't have Ana, and that's the worst part. I close my eyes, swallowing against the sudden tightness in my throat. I miss my girl with an intensity that nearly steals my breath. Being away from her this long has been nothing short of slow torture.

"Morning."

I look up as Pavel steps into the kitchen, already dressed for the day. His sharp navy suit is tailored to perfection, his tie in a Windsor knot, his shirt starched and crisp. He looks good as far as fashion goes, but his eyes look exhausted, so much so that it catches me off guard. He's been running himself ragged.

"Heading out?" I ask, taking a sip of coffee.

His lips twitch slightly, like he knows I'm fishing, but he doesn't call me out on it.

"Meetings," he says simply.

I nod casually, pretending not to care, hiding the fact that I wish he would stay. He crosses the kitchen in a few long strides, planting a chaste kiss on my cheek. Soft. Routine.

"Don't get into trouble while I'm gone."

"No promises."

He chuckles, the sound low and genuine, then straightens, adjusting his cuffs before heading for the door. And just like that, he's gone.

I don't move right away, waiting to hear the sound of the elevator doors closing. I give it another few minutes, just to be safe, before slipping back into my room, grabbing my bag and phone. This is what has become routine now, a carefully crafted lie.

I step into the elevator, taking it down to the underground garage. The doors slide open, and soon I'm stepping out onto the streets of Tribeca—the place I now call home.

Everything about this part of Manhattan screams wealth. Glass-and-steel skyscrapers, luxury storefronts, the scent of espresso coming from the boutique cafes. The sidewalks are always clean, the streets always patrolled. It's the kind of place where money moves silently, where power hums just beneath the surface. It's beautiful.

And it's suffocating.

As I slip into the back of one of our cars, the driver looks at me in the rearview mirror. "Going to visit your brothers today, Mrs. Fetisova?"

"Yes, Maxim, thank you." We pull away from the towering skyline of Lower Manhattan, heading northwest, weaving through the streets until we reach Carroll Gardens. Then, the shift is instantaneous. Carroll Gardens is old New York: brick townhouses, tree-lined streets, brownstones that have stood the test of time. It's charming in a way that Tribeca will never be. Warm, familiar, lived-in.

We slow in front of a modest but well-kept brownstone, its windows lined with flower boxes, its red front door slightly faded from the sun. Big hedges block the windows from view—Vlad's way of keeping prying eyes from seeing inside.

My heart clenches. *This* is home.

I slip out of the town car and make my way up the stone steps. My fingers hover over the brass handle for just a second before pushing the door open. The driver and guard wait for me in the car, just as they have done on previous visits.

The warmth and nostalgia of the house wraps around me instantly. The faint smell of vanilla and sugar lingers in the air, a scent I've missed more than I realized. I barely have time to close the door behind me before I hear the sound of small feet padding against the wooden floor, followed by a squeal of joy.

"Mama!"

She's in my arms within seconds. A blur of dark curls and pink crashes into me, tiny arms wrapping around my waist. Ana nearly knocks me off my feet with the force of her hug. I love it, but it's a reminder of how quickly she's growing up, how every day I spend away from her is a day I miss seeing it happen.

I exhale sharply, my heart clenching as I scoop her up, burying my face in her hair.

"I missed you," she says, her voice muffled against my neck.

I hold her tighter. "I missed you more, baby."

She pulls back just enough to look at me, her big brown eyes filled with a question I already know is coming. "When are you coming home for good?"

A lump forms in my throat. How am I supposed to answer that? I smooth a hand over her curls, pressing a kiss to her forehead. "Soon, my love."

But I know that might not be true.

I hear the sound of heels clicking against the hardwood. I look up to see Camille Barbier watching us from the doorway. Camille is poised, polished, and effortlessly chic, like every French woman seems to be. She wears tailored slacks and a silk blouse. Her dark hair is swept into a simple, but elegant twist. She's in her mid-thirties and has an air of effortless sophistication, but there's warmth beneath it, a genuine fondness for Ana.

Camille has been with us since the day Ana was born. She's a little bit of everything—a tutor, a nanny, a guardian when I can't be here. She homeschools Ana, gives her structure, and keeps her safe. Camille, along with Vlad and Piotr, have been looking after Ana since I married Pavel.

"Mommy!" Ana says. "I want to show you something I drew!" With that, she's off, leaving me and Camille alone.

"Kat," she says in greeting, her French accent apparent. "*Ça va?*"

Ça va means "How's it going?" in French. She already knows the answer to that.

"Same," I reply. "I'm only a couple of miles away, but it feels like I'm in another state. How's she been?"

Camille shifts her weight from one foot to the other. "She's been asking for you every day. I don't think she knows quite what to make of her *maman* not being around as much as she used to."

"I know," I say, a sadness in my voice. I think about how Ana hugged me when I first walked in. She held on for dear life, like she would never let me go. The guilt feels overwhelming, threatening to consume me.

Camille's lips press together, as if weighing her words before speaking. She doesn't approve of this arrangement—of me being gone while Ana stays here with Piotr and Vlad. But she never speaks against it outright. She knows better than to question the Bratva's decisions.

"It shouldn't be much longer," I say.

"Hopefully not. A girl needs her mother."

With that, Ana returns, a picture in her hands. "Look, Mommy!"

Camille walks forward, gently smoothing the bow on Ana's dress. "You two have a lot to catch up on. I'll let you be."

"*Merci*, Camille," I say.

She gives me a small smile before slipping out, her heels clicking with quiet finality.

Ana seems to forget all about the picture. It falls to the floor as she comes over for another hug.

"I really miss you, Mama."

I swallow the lump in my throat, hating how much time I've lost.

"I miss you too, baby," I whisper, tightening my hold on her.

"I don't want you to leave again."

I don't know what to say. I can't promise her that I'm coming back anytime soon. As long as Pavel lives, as long as *her father* lives, I have to be apart from her.

Ana lets go, stepping back. "Mommy, can you make me lunch?"

"I'd love to."

For the next hour, I lose myself in the comfort of her presence. We make *pelmeni* together, her favorite. The dough is messy, and she gets more flour on herself than in the bowl, but I don't care. She chatters the entire time, telling me stories about her lessons, her little fingers working carefully as I show her how to fold the dumplings properly.

When the food is ready, we sit down together at the kitchen table. She digs in with a happy sigh, her little feet swinging beneath her chair.

"I'm learning French," she announces proudly between bites, stuffing another *pelmeni* into her mouth.

I smile, gently brushing a loose curl from her cheek. "I know, baby. How's it going?"

Ana scowls. "Camille won't let me speak Russian during lessons."

I chuckle. "She's trying to get you to focus on French during that time, my love."

"But sometimes I forget the words. And she makes me look them up. It's mean."

I press my lips together to keep from laughing. "It's not mean. It's how you learn."

She sighs dramatically, then quickly brightens. "I know some words now! Do you want to hear?"

"Of course."

She sits up straighter, her little face turning serious. *"Je m'appelle* Ana," she says carefully, then grins. "That means, my name is Ana."

I smile. *"Très bien, mon amour."*

Ana giggles, then scrunches up her face in concentration. *"Je t'aime ma maman!"*

My heart melts. "And what does that mean?"

I already know the answer, I just want to hear her say it.

She beams at me. "I love my mama."

I pull her into my arms, kissing her forehead. "I love you too, my sweet girl. More than anything."

She hums happily, snuggling against me. "You say it now, Mama."

I whisper the words in French against her hair, holding her close, inhaling the warm, sweet scent of her. She loves to learn, to prove she's capable, just like me when I was younger. The tenderness of the moment fills me; a rare peace settling within my chest. That is, until the door opens and footsteps approach from behind. I don't have to turn around to know who it is. The tension in the air tells me before I even see him.

"Uncle Piotr!" Ana exclaims, her face beaming.

"There's my little muffin!" Piotr strides over, scooping my daughter into his arms. With his free hand, he grabs a *pelmeni* and pops it into his mouth. I stay quiet, and he doesn't fail to notice.

"Am I interrupting?"

"What are you doing here?"

He laughs. "I live here, remember? Part of the arrangement."

"Fair enough. But don't you have family business to attend to?"

The truth of the matter is, I want to spend time with my daughter—alone. The look on Piotr's face, knowing and supercilious, suggests he stopped by for another reason besides saying hi to his sister.

"This right here is the only family business I care about at the moment." He places a kiss on Ana's forehead, then sets her down before settling into the chair across from me. "I told the guards to let me know when you come over."

My spine stiffens. That's new.

"And why is that? Are you keeping tabs on me?"

"No," he says firmly, crossing his arms. "But if you're going to be pulling a stunt where you slip away, then discreetly drop by for visits—something I don't recommend, by the way—I want to know when it happens."

I open my mouth to respond, but I don't get the chance.

Ana picks up on the atmospheric shift in the room, her little face scrunching as she looks between us. "Are you mad at each other?"

I force a soft smile, reaching for her hand. "No, sweetheart. Everything's fine."

She doesn't look convinced. She's too perceptive for that.

Before she can ask anything else, however, Camille appears in the doorway. "Ana, time to get ready for ballet."

Ana gasps, suddenly remembering. She scrambles out of her chair, excitement replacing her earlier concern. "Mama, my recital is in three weeks! You're going to be there, right?"

Another lump rises in my throat. I've lost count at how many I've experienced since being here. Three weeks. Her father will be dead by then, and I'll be back with her, where I belong.

I nod, forcing a smile onto my lips. "Of course, my love."

She beams, pressing a quick kiss to my cheek before dashing off with Camille to get dressed for ballet class. She stops and looks back. "Love you, Mama!"

I watch her go, a twisting ache forming deep in my chest. God, I hate leaving her. I need to end this. But not in the way Piotr wants me to.

"Is she going alone?" I ask once she's out of earshot. "I mean, with anyone besides Camille?"

Piotr cocks his head to the side. "Are you asking if Ana is protected? If she needs guards?"

I glance at him, wary. "Of course I am, and of course she does. She's my daughter."

Piotr leans back in his chair, watching me. "She's safe at all times."

That should reassure me, but it doesn't. I don't trust him anymore. I say nothing. Instead, I nod, then stand up, reaching for my purse on the counter.

"Going so soon?" he asks.

"Yes. I need to get back before Pavel does. I don't want him asking questions."

"I understand. But you and I need to chat before you leave."

I stop cold, my fingers tightening around my purse.

"A chat? About what?"

"Just come to my office; we can talk in there."

"Your office?"

He grins. "I set myself up in one of the spare bedrooms. It looks pretty good, if I do say so myself. Come on."

Piotr doesn't wait to see if I follow. He just expects me to, leaving the kitchen without another word.

I stare after him for a long moment, a slow burn of irritation creeping up my spine.

I follow with a bitterness in my throat I can't stand to swallow.

CHAPTER 15

KAT

"Come in, dear sister."

Piotr's office is exactly what I expected—cold, sterile, and devoid of any personality. Everything about it is designed to intimidate, without an ounce of comfort. A massive desk dominates the space, its polished surface reflecting the overhead lighting.

"Have a seat," he says, sweeping his hand toward a pair of chairs in front of his desk.

The chairs are small and uncomfortable, meant to make whoever sits in them feel insignificant and uneasy. I roll my eyes.

Piotr slides into the large, cozy, leather chair behind his desk. He places his feet up, steepling his hands over his chest. He wants me to feel like I'm beneath him. I don't give him the satisfaction.

Instead of taking one of the tiny chairs, I stroll right past them, my heels clicking softly against the floor as I make my way to the bar in the corner. A decanter of expensive whiskey sits on a glass shelf beside crystal tumblers. I pour myself a generous drink, swirling the amber liquid lazily. I don't offer him one.

Piotr's lips curl slightly, amusement flickering in his eyes. He knows exactly what I'm doing. He lets me have my little moment and doesn't call me out on it.

I carry the tumbler over to the couch on the other side of the room, settling into the cushions with a deliberate ease and heavy sigh. If he wants to play games, I'll play them, too.

His gaze hardens for a quick second, clearly irritated that I didn't squeeze myself into one of the little "guest" chairs. But his expression soon turns to one of amusement as he leans back in his seat, drumming his fingers on the armrest. If he wants me to squirm, I'm not going to give him the satisfaction.

The amusement is soon replaced with a hard sternness. Time to get down to business.

"For the second time, Katerina, why isn't he dead?"

He says it so casually, as if he's asking me why I forgot to pick up milk from the store, instead of why I haven't killed my husband. My stomach twists in disgust, but I don't let it show. Instead, I lift a brow, slowly tracing the rim of my glass with my finger as if I'm bored.

"Because I don't think the Fetisovs are responsible." I say it with a steady voice, but inside, my pulse is hammering. I'm not a hundred percent certain they're innocent. I don't know anything for sure. I'm going with my gut.

Piotr's expression doesn't shift, other than a slight narrowing of his eyes. He stops drumming his fingers on the armrest for half a second before resuming a slow, steady beat. He doesn't like my answer.

Good.

"I want to do a little digging before I murder a man you used to call your best friend," I continue, keeping my voice calm and even.

Piotr exhales sharply through his nose, shaking his head. "This is ridiculous. We've had this planned for months. And don't forget, that so-called 'best friend' is the person who ordered the hit on our parents."

I cock my head to the side. "And how do you know that, exactly?"

His jaw tightens. "Everyone knows that," he says flatly, as if that's supposed to be enough to convince me.

I scoff, a humorless laugh escaping before I can stop it. "That's not proof, Piotr. That's gossip, hearsay."

Something flashes in his eyes. Annoyance? Frustration? Whatever it is, it vanishes almost instantly.

"What the hell is this?" he asks. "You were dead set on this plan with me, now you're having second thoughts?" An aggravated sigh follows. "I knew it was a fucking mistake to have you be the one who did the deed. You're too close to him, always have been. You're too soft."

Soft? Describing me as soft simply pisses me off.

The door swings open before I can respond, and Vlad steps in. His glare sweeps between us, reading the tension instantly.

"What's going on? Are the two of you having a meeting that I'm not a part of?"

Piotr doesn't hesitate before speaking. He doesn't even glance my way before replying to our brother. "Kat lacks the guts to move forward with our plan. We may need to resort to other measures."

I stiffen. The anger that had been simmering beneath my skin finally spills over. I stand and step toward Piotr's desk, planting my hands on the polished surface, leaning in. "Excuse me?"

Piotr shrugs, as if my reaction doesn't faze him. "If you won't do it, I'll find someone who will."

Rage ignites in my chest. "You don't get to decide that," I snap.

Piotr smirks. "Don't I?"

My hands tighten into fists. "I am not a cold-blooded killer, Piotr. I won't kill a man without proof, without a damn good reason."

He tilts his head, looking at me like I've now become a problem that needs to be solved. I can tell he's pissed, barely holding it together.

"Where the hell is this coming from?" he asks, his voice rising. "While we were formulating the plan, you were chomping at the goddamn bit to see Pavel dead. In fact, you were adamant about being the one to do it. And now, suddenly, you're getting cold feet and making excuses."

He has me there. I wasn't a helpless little bystander in the plan. I'd helped put it together, promised to see it through. I purse my lips. "I just want to be certain, that's all."

The air in the room is thick, suffocating. A silent battle waged in glares and clenched fists.

Vlad clears his throat, stepping between us. "Enough," he says firmly, "both of you."

Piotr leans back in his chair once again, exhaling loudly as if we've exhausted him. "This was never supposed to be this complicated. He should already be dead."

Vlad's eyes flick to me. "I think it was always going to be complicated."

Piotr scoffs, shaking his head. "No, she's just making it that way."

I inhale sharply, clenching my teeth to keep from screaming. Piotr acts like this is all so simple. As if taking a life—taking *this* life, in particular—is just another business transaction. But it isn't. Not for me. Not for Vlad, either, apparently.

Vlad crosses his arms over his chest, his jaw tight. "She wants time," he says. "Give it to her."

Piotr levels him with a cold stare. "Are you kidding? She doesn't deserve more time. If you ask me, she's grown weak. She's simply stalling."

"Screw you, Piotr," I shoot back.

Piotr looks at me with that infuriatingly calm and amused expression. "I have proof."

My heart kicks up. Finally. "Then show me," I challenge.

His smirk is slow and condescending. "I can't. The man who told me died three years ago."

The rush of anticipation that had flared turns to ash. I laugh. I can't help it. The situation is so ridiculous that all I can do is laugh. Even Vlad's serious expression cracks for a moment.

"What's so goddamn funny?" he asks.

"That's not proof, Piotr, that's a fucking rumor from a dead man."

His gaze hardens.

I say, "Like I told you, I'm going to do some digging, whether you like it or not."

Piotr's gaze darkens, his jaw tightening. "You'll do what you're told."

"No, I won't." The air ignites, the disparities between us erupting in an instant.

Piotr slams his fist on the desk as he stands, his chair tipping backward. "You think this is some kind of game, Kat? You think this is about feelings?"

I step closer, refusing to back down. "I think you're reckless. I think you're dragging us into a war without any goddamn proof."

His eyes burn into mine, unflinching. "I think you're weak and scared."

"And I think you're desperate."

His nostrils flare. "Everything I do, I do for this family."

I scoff. "Is that what you tell yourself? That this is about family, about justice? This is about you and the power you crave, Piotr, nothing more."

He stares me down, his voice quiet as he says, "He killed our parents."

"You don't know that for sure!" I snap, my voice rising.

"I know enough."

"You know nothing," I spit back, closing the distance between us. "You want to talk about weakness? About loyalty? You're using Dad's death as an excuse to justify your cruelty, your desire for power."

His expression turns cold. "Watch your mouth."

I ignore him, pressing forward, my voice laced with venom. "You're not a leader like he was. You don't inspire loyalty, Piotr. You demand obedience."

The words hit their mark. I can see it in his eyes.

For the first time, he doesn't have a response. His lip curls in disgust. "You're a traitor to this family, and you're a coward."

The words cut deep, but not because I believe them. It proves exactly what I've always known: Piotr doesn't want a sister; he wants a soldier.

Before I can lash back, Vlad slams his palm against the wall. "Enough!"

Silence crashes over us like a tidal wave.

I turn to Vlad, breathing hard, my chest rising and falling rapidly. He stands between us now, his eyes hard, jaw set. He's the only thing keeping Piotr and me from tearing each other apart. Piotr stares down Vlad but he doesn't flinch.

"I think she at least deserves the chance to find the truth. Once this is done, it's done. And it's not just a matter of feeling bad for poor Pavel. His death will put into motion events that we won't be able to undo. We need to get this right."

Piotr's jaw flexes, but he doesn't argue.

Vlad exhales slowly. "Give her the time she's asking for."

Piotr doesn't respond.

"Come on," Vlad says. "The longer she keeps him alive, the more intel she could come across."

That gets Piotr's attention. Vlad, sensing that he's onto something, continues. "When Pavel's dead, his Bratva is going to fall into total chaos. Every family in the city is going to try to bite off a piece of what he's got in the aftermath. It's not just about killing him, it's about timing. The more information we gather, the better positioned we'll be to take advantage of what happens once word spreads that he's gone."

"We're not going to get another chance like this," I add. "Might as well take advantage of it."

Piotr stares at me, his fingers tapping on the polished wood of his desk. "Two weeks."

His voice is clipped. Final. "Not a day longer. You'd better make good use of the extra time. Find out everything you can about his operations."

I want to argue for more than two weeks. I need more than that. But I know Piotr and I know that's all I'm going to get.

Grudgingly, I nod. "Fine."

His lips twitch slightly, like he knows how much I hate agreeing with him. I turn to Vlad, softening just slightly. "Thank you."

He nods, reaching for my hand and squeezing it briefly before I press a kiss to his cheek.

I turn to leave, my hand already curling around the doorknob, desperate to get away from Piotr before I say something I can't take back.

But just as I start to open the door, Piotr speaks. "Your duty is still to this family, Katerina."

I don't turn around. Instead, I keep my hand on the doorknob, my fingers tightening around the cool metal. Then, without looking back, I say the only thing I know for certain. "My loyalty lies with those who are loyal to me."

Silence.

I can feel Piotr's stare. Heavy. Assessing. Calculating. He's deciding something, testing me.

I open the door and step out, asking myself the question I should have been asking all along:

Who is Piotr truly loyal to?

CHAPTER 16

PAVEL

One week later...

"Report."

Ivan and Dima stand before me, their postures rigid. They don't waste time with pleasantries.

"Nothing unusual," Ivan says. "No unknown contacts, no signs of surveillance, no attempts to approach her."

Dima nods. "She visits the Andreev home every few days, stays a few hours, then comes home."

"Good. Keep it that way," I order. "If anyone so much as looks in her direction, I want to know. If her routine changes in any way, I want to know. Immediately."

"Yes, Boss," Ivan says.

I drum my fingers against my desk, considering. "She's not meeting with anyone outside her family?"

Dima shakes his head. "Not that we've seen."

"We could learn more if you want to post us on twenty-four-hour surveillance. We could branch out—" Ivan starts.

I shake my head, putting a hand up to stop him. It's tempting, but Kat's the priority.

"That's not necessary. Stay with my wife; make sure she's safe."

"Understood," Ivan replies.

I nod once and turn away, dismissing them. The door closes, and I take a moment to savor the silence, allowing my mind to unspool. Kat's keeping to a predictable routine. That should reassure me, but instead, it only fuels my curiosity. She had friends when we were together before, yet she's not meeting with any of them. Has she lost touch?

I hardly see her these days. We haven't been alone together in weeks. It's driving me to near insanity.

Time keeps moving forward. She's been in my home for over a month now, and despite the distance between us, I've grown fond of having her near. I'm used to waking up with her beside me, even if I don't touch her, used to the scent of her lingering on the sheets, to hearing her voice somewhere in the penthouse. I tell myself that it's simply habit, nothing more. But I know better.

I'm falling for her, but I don't know where she stands.

With that thought circling my mind, I head toward her office. Our bedroom is shared, but I wanted her to have a space of her own in this place. *Our* place. I like the way that sounds, like she belongs here, like she belongs to me.

The door is slightly ajar. I step closer, pausing when I see her.

The office is unmistakably hers. The walls are lined with bookshelves filled with a mix of literature and business titles. A plush rug covers the hardwood floor, an ivory velvet couch with oversized deep green throw pillows sits in the corner.

A touch of elegance, just like her. There are small hints of her personality everywhere—a crystal vase with fresh flowers on the coffee table, a framed photo of her and her brothers on one of the shelves, a white leather ergonomic chair behind her desk.

And that's where she is, sitting at her desk, completely unaware of my presence.

Fuck, she's beautiful.

Her dark hair is loosely pinned back. Her lips are slightly parted as she focuses on the computer screen, her brows furrowed in concentration. The soft lamplight casts a warm glow on her skin, making her look almost ethereal.

I should say something. Instead, I just watch her, taking in the way she unconsciously bites her lower lip as she reads something on the screen; the way her delicate fingers hover over the keyboard before she finally types; the way her chest rises and falls steadily, her fitted silk blouse clinging to the curves that have haunted me since the first time I touched her.

I clear my throat quietly, not wanting to startle her.

She looks up, and the moment our eyes meet, she smiles.

My heart seizes.

She closes the laptop and stretches, arching her back.

"Work or pleasure?" I ask.

"Just doing some reading," she replies. "Nothing important."

I step fully into the room, my gaze drifting downward, taking in the way the soft silk of her shirt pulls tight over her chest, the fabric straining against the full curves of her breasts. My eyes linger, drawn to the faint press of her nipples through the thin material.

Right then, I know what I want, what I need. I stride forward, shutting the door behind me. The corner of her mouth lifts slightly, amusement flickering in her gaze as she watches me approach. She knows what's coming.

And she wants it, too.

In three long strides, I'm close enough to touch her. My fingers glide along her jaw, tilting her face up to mine. "How about a little break?"

Her lips twitch. "No time for that."

I hum, my thumb tracing along the corner of her mouth. "And now?"

I move my thumb over her lips. She closes her eyes and opens her mouth before wrapping her lips around it, licking and sucking it playfully. I get hard right away. I slip my thumb out.

She tilts her head then sighs. "That depends. Are you going to keep looking at my tits like that, or are you going to do something about it?"

A low growl rumbles in my throat. She always knows how to get me going, knows exactly what she's doing. I answer her by pulling her to her feet and capturing her mouth, my lips crushing against hers. She gasps as her hands slide up my chest, her fingers gripping the fabric of my shirt, pulling me closer.

I deepen the kiss, my tongue sweeping into her mouth, tasting her, drinking her in, watching her.

She moans, her body melting into mine, but when I slide my hands down to her waist, she pulls back just enough to whisper against my lips. "You're still staring," she murmurs, teasing.

"Can you blame me?" My voice is rough, full of heat. "You're fucking perfect."

She gives a soft little laugh, her cheeks flushing just a little. She likes it when I tell her that.

I slide my hands lower, gripping her hips, pressing her back against the desk. "You like distracting me, don't you?"

She leans in, her lips brushing against my jaw, giving it a soft nibble. "Hey, you're the one who came into *my* office."

"Yeah, I suppose I did."

I lift her onto the desk, pushing her knees apart and stepping between them. I lean in, my lips grazing the shell of her ear, my voice dropping to a murmur. "Let's see how much work you get done now, *moya zhena*."

I don't take my time.

I devour her.

Her moan vibrates against my lips, only making me hungrier. My hands move to her waist, lifting her effortlessly. She squeals as I spin us, setting her down on the couch.

I kneel in front of her, pushing her thighs apart, my hands sliding up the soft skin. Her chest rises and falls rapidly in eager anticipation.

"I've barely seen you lately," I say, kissing the inside of her knee.

"I've been busy."

"So have I. But right now, I don't give a fuck about anything else but this."

Her breath shudders as I push her skirt up higher, exposing more of her to me.

"Oh God…"

"Tell me you want this."

She hesitates. I grip her thighs, my thumbs brushing against the sensitive skin. "Tell me, Kat."

Her lips part. Her voice is barely above a whisper. "I want this."

That's all I need. I slide my hands beneath her lace panties, hooking my fingers under the delicate fabric and dragging them down her legs, tossing them aside.

She's already wet.

I grip her thighs tighter as I lower my mouth to her. The first flick of my tongue makes her jerk. The second makes her moan with pleasure. I don't rush. I take my time, savoring her essence, every breathless sound, every tremble of her body as I pleasure her.

I tease. I taste. I feast.

She writhes beneath me, hands fisting into my hair, hips arching toward my mouth.

"Pavel," she gasps.

I answer by sucking her clit.

She falls apart so beautifully. I don't stop until she's begging, trembling, breathless. I pull away, staring down at her flushed, panting form.

"Your turn," she says, reaching for my belt.

She slides off the couch, her knees hitting the plush rug beneath her. Her hands skim up my thighs, slow, deliberate, nails barely scraping the fabric of my pants as she looks up at me. She holds my gaze as she undoes the buckle with practiced ease, then slowly unzips my slacks. The control in her movements is maddening, her fingers grazing my skin just enough to send heat coursing through my veins.

I lift myself up onto the couch, watching her, letting her take her time.

She palms me through my boxer briefs first, her touch light, teasing, a ghost of pressure that makes my muscles clench. She presses a soft kiss against my clothed length, her lips warm through the fabric, and, *fuck*, I nearly lose it right there.

"Kat," I growl in warning, my fingers sinking into her hair.

She smirks against me, loving that I'm already unraveling for her. She hooks her fingers into the waistband of my briefs and drags them down, freeing me. My cock is already hard, aching, the tip slick with precum, desperate for her mouth.

When she finally takes me into her hand, stroking once—slow, tight, perfect—I curse under my breath. She doesn't rush; she teases.

Her thumb swipes back and forth over the head before leaning in and licking a slow, obscene stripe along the underside of my length. My grip tightens in her hair. Then, with a wicked glint in her eyes, she wraps her lips around me and sinks down.

A guttural groan rumbles in my chest as I watch her take me deeper, her tongue pressing against the thick vein along my shaft, her mouth so goddamn hot and wet around me, it's maddening.

"Fuck," I bite out, my head tipping back for a brief second before I force myself to look down at her again.

"Look at me," I order.

She does.

The sight of her on her knees, her lips stretched around my cock, her eyes locked on mine, nearly shatters me. I flex my hips slightly, pushing deeper, groaning as she takes it, as she hollows her cheeks, sucking harder.

"Jesus, Kat."

I fist her hair tighter, guiding her, controlling the pace. She lets me, but she's just as much in control as I am. She flicks her tongue just right, moaning around me in a way that sends vibrations up my spine, making my whole body coil tightly.

I'm getting close to the edge. Right fucking there. And she knows it.

She slows, dragging her lips over me torturously, pulling back until only the head of my cock is in her mouth, her tongue flicking against the tip. My breath shudders. My muscles lock. I'm so goddamn close.

Then she takes me deep again, humming low in her throat, and I yank her off of me. She gasps, eyes wide, lips slick, her breath coming fast. I can still feel the ghost of her mouth on me, the chasm of pleasure she nearly dragged me into.

"Enough," I rasp, dragging her to her feet. I slide my hand up her body, cupping her breast through her blouse, my thumb brushing over her hard nipple. She presses her body into mine.

"You like teasing me, don't you?"

Her fingers clutch at my shoulders, her breath uneven. "Maybe."

I smirk, nipping at the sensitive skin just below her jaw. "Then it's only fair I return the favor."

I slide my hands down, gripping the backs of her thighs, lifting her up. She wraps her legs around my waist. I step toward the desk, clearing it with a sweep of my arm. Papers scatter, and a pen clatters to the floor before I set her down. She's so ready for me.

Desperate. Dripping.

I'm going to make sure she knows exactly who she belongs to before this night is over. I unbutton her blouse, pushing the fabric from her shoulders, dragging my lips down the column of her throat, along the soft curve of her breast. She moans.

"Tell me what you want, Kat."

She swallows hard, her fingers trailing through my hair.

"You," she whispers.

I press my palm between her thighs before sinking into her.

CHAPTER 17

KAT

Pavel doesn't waste a second. One moment, I'm on my knees in front of him, the next, he's setting me on the desk, plunging his cock into me. He grips my hips, pulling me to him, pushing himself into me deep and fast.

"You're mine," he growls, his breath hot against my ear. His fingers press into my skin, pinning me in place. He thrusts into me again and again, hard and unforgiving.

I cry out, my fingers gripping the desk, my pussy stretching around him. He's relentless, each push of his hips sending shock waves through me. "Pavel."

"Say it again."

His hand slides up my spine then fists into my hair, tugging my head back. I feel exposed, completely at his mercy. I love it.

"You like this, don't you?" His voice is a dark rasp, full of satisfaction, full of ownership.

I don't answer fast enough.

Smack.

A sharp slap lands against my ass, making me jolt, my walls clenching tighter around him. He growls, his grip tightening. "Fuck, you feel that? How tight you get when I put you in your place?"

A breathless whimper escapes me.

Yes. I feel everything.

I try to move, try to roll my hips to meet his thrusts, but he doesn't let me. His hands hold me still, forcing me to take it the way he wants to give it. Deep. Dominating. Merciless.

Every inch of me is on fire.

"Answer me, Kat."

"Yes. God, yes."

He chuckles before picking up the pace, fucking me harder, deeper. Each drive of his hips makes me gasp, every stroke brushing over the spot that makes my vision blur.

"I can feel you," he bites out, his fingers sinking into my hips. "You're going to come for me, aren't you?"

I breathe his name as I come hard and fast, my body clenching tight around him, pulling him with me. His growl is low and guttural, vibrating through my bones as he thrusts one last time, causing a thundering orgasm throughout my body.

Afterward, he doesn't let go. Doesn't move. He stays there, his weight pressing down on me, keeping me exactly where he wants me. Oddly, I don't want to move either. Because I know, no matter how much I try to deny it, I love the way he owns me.

Before I can catch my breath, my body still pulsing around him, Pavel lifts me up, turning me in one swift motion until I'm bent over in front of him, his cock still thick and hard. A helpless moan slips from my lips as I grind into him, his hands gripping my waist, holding me steady, making me feel every inch of him as he plunges back in.

His hand moves to my throat, gripping but not squeezing, applying just enough pressure to still me.

"You take what I give you, understand?" he says, his thumb stroking my pulse, feeling it race beneath his touch. "Not the other way around."

I shudder at his words, surprised at my own reaction to his dominance. His free hand slides around me, fingers teasing over my already swollen clit. I moan, bucking into him, gripping the desk with everything I've got.

"That's it," he says. "You love this, don't you? You love when I fuck you from behind."

His other hand moves from my throat to my breast, squeezing it, teasing my nipple. He guides me, pulling me closer to him by the hips, making me take him deeper, harder. I feel like I'm coming apart at the seams, losing myself completely.

"Come for me again," he orders.

With a shattered cry, I do, my back arching, my entire body clenching as he holds me still, forcing me to take every second of it. I feel like I'm a marionette and he's pulling the strings. It's at this moment that I know I'll give him anything he wants.

Because I want to.

Before my orgasm fades, he moves me back to the couch. He places me onto my back and slides inside again, filling me in the way only he can, the way I crave, that way I *need*. Pavel stays inside me, his body heavy over mine, his weight pressing me deep into the plush couch. His skin is hot and damp where it meets mine, his breath uneven against my cheek. But he doesn't make any move to pull away.

Instead, he shifts slightly, propping himself up on his elbows, his body still flush against mine. His hands frame my face, his thumbs brushing over my cheekbones with a tenderness that surprises me. My heart stumbles in my chest. I don't know what to do with this version of him—the one that isn't all hard edges and rough demands. This version is soft and tender, ultimately making him even more dangerous, when it comes to my heart.

Pavel tilts his head, his blue eyes locked on mine, studying me like he's trying to figure me out. He smirks.

"Did I break you, Katerina?" His voice is husky, still thick with lust, but there's a warmth in it.

I scoff, trying to ignore the way my stomach flutters at the way he says my name. "You wish."

His smirk widens. He rolls his hips just slightly, still buried deep inside me. I gasp, my fingers tightening on his biceps. "Oh!"

He hums in a smug way, dragging his nose along my jaw before pressing a slow, lazy kiss to my lips. "Where's all that attitude? All that fire?"

I lift my chin defiantly. "It's still here."

He chuckles, pressing another kiss to my throat, his lips lingering over my pulse. "Mmm, that's good." Another slow thrust, deep and teasing, making me shudder. His expression shifts slightly, his voice dropping lower. "I like seeing you like this."

I swallow hard. "Like what?"

He drags his lips over my collarbone, his hips shifting just enough to make me squirm. "Relaxed," he murmurs. "Satisfied." He presses a kiss just above my breast, then looks me in the eye. "Mine."

A sharp ache blooms in my chest.

Not fair.

This is supposed to be about sex, power, control. Not this. Not him whispering sweet things that make me melt like a stick of butter. I lift my chin, narrowing my eyes. "I'm not yours."

Pavel's eyes darken into something dangerous. He leans in, his voice a quiet murmur as his nose skims mine. "No?"

I open my mouth to argue but he moves again, a slow, deep thrust that leaves me breathless. He watches me, drinking in my reaction, smug and knowing. Then, with a wicked smirk, he rolls his hips again. "Feels like you are."

His arms stay tight against my sides, strong and solid, anchoring me in a way I didn't expect. His breath is slow and steady, like a feather against my temple. His fingers stroke my cheek, a lazy, soothing motion that makes my eyelids grow heavy. I can feel his heartbeat against my own. Strong. Certain. Unshaken.

He murmurs something in Russian, then chuckles, low and rough, the sound rumbling through his chest.

I frown, lifting my head just enough to look at him. "What did you just say?"

His lips twitch, the corners lifting in an amused, knowing smirk. Smug. Teasing.

I narrow my eyes. "Pavel."

He hums, dragging his fingers through my hair, twirling a loose strand around his finger as he studies me. "I said you look beautiful when you're completely ruined."

Heat licks up my spine, pooling low in my stomach. I swat at his arm, scowling. "You are insufferable."

He grins. "I can tell you're thinking too much," he replies after a few seconds.

"You don't think enough."

His smirk fades slightly, replaced by something more serious. "I think about a lot of things, Kat." His voice is softer now, and when his fingers slide back up in my hair, I lean into his touch without hesitation. "I think about you."

I swallow hard, my throat tightening at his words. I know I shouldn't ask the next question, but I do anyway. "What exactly do you think about?"

His fingers tighten ever so slightly, his jaw clenching before he answers. "I think about the way you feel in my arms. I think about how good you taste. How fucking perfect you are when you come for me."

I inhale sharply, my pulse racing, but he isn't finished.

"I think about the way you look at me when you don't think I see it." His thumb brushes over my lips, slow and deliberate. "Like you want this just as much as I do."

I do.

Good God, I do.

But I can't say it. I won't say it. Because this wasn't supposed to happen. I shift, pressing my face against his chest, closing my eyes. "You're so full of yourself."

He chuckles as he wraps his arms around me, pulling me closer. "I meant every word."

I don't know what to say to that. Suddenly, the room feels too small, the weight of everything said, as well as everything unsaid, pressing down on me. He moves again, and I let myself go. I lock my legs around his hips, pulling him deeper inside. A few more thrusts, and I'm tipping over the edge again, with him right alongside me.

I'm taken back to the night we made Ana.

I can't help but wonder what would have happened if I'd never left.

CHAPTER 18

PAVEL

I roll my sleeves up, then push aside the paperwork in front of me. My mind isn't on numbers or business. It's on Kat.

Manhattan stretches into the distance beyond the tall windows of my office. The sky is a sheet of slate-gray clouds. I know there's a war brewing. But all I can think about is my wife. She's in my home, in my bed, but I don't know if she's truly mine.

I try to keep my Bratva dealings separate from her. I don't want her involved in that part of my world any more than she needs to be. But she *is* Bratva. Whether she likes it or not, whether she *admits* it or not, her allegiance is still tied to the Andreev name. And while I can tell she cares for me, I also know that loyalty in our world is never simple.

She's been visiting her brothers' house regularly. Too regularly. And though my men report nothing suspicious, I can't shake the feeling that something is off. I want to trust her, but I don't.

The knock at my door is sharp. There's a problem. I can feel it.

"Come in," I call out, leaning back in my chair, bracing myself.

Nikolai enters, his expression serious and controlled. He's a man used to handling bad news, and I can tell he has some to share.

"We have a situation."

I sigh. Of course we do. "Go on."

"There are rumors going around about the Andreevs."

"What kind of rumors?"

"Ones that suggest Piotr's behind the attacks."

I shift my weight in my seat. Such news isn't surprising. Even though he has professed loyalty all these years, I've begun to question his sincerity. "Who's talking?" I ask.

"Sources from the street. A few mid-level guys. No one big enough to confirm yet."

I nod, considering the information. If these whispers are making their way down the ranks, then it means the truth—whatever it may be—is close to surfacing.

Piotr has been avoiding me lately. Every time I try to set up a meeting to finalize the merger, he conveniently has somewhere else to be, offering lame excuses about handling the chaos and cleaning up the mess from the attacks. I'm starting to believe the chaos and the mess is exactly what he wanted.

I lace my fingers together, resting my chin on my knuckles. "If it's true," I say, "then what's his angle?"

Nikolai doesn't hesitate. "Power."

Power. Control. The same things every man at the top of the Bratva pyramid wants. But Piotr already has power. He has his father's seat. He has his own army. But he also has me, and therein lies the problem.

I've been discreetly asking questions about the former Andreev *pakhan's* death, but every road leads me to nowhere. The way Piotr took control so quickly after his parents' accident. It seemed too clean, too convenient.

I drum my fingers against the desk. I need answers. I could go to Vlad, but that would be a violation, not to mention that circumventing Piotr would lay my motivations—and my suspicions—bare.

I glance up at Nikolai. "What else?"

His expression sharpens. "I might have something, a new lead."

I arch a brow. Interesting.

"Tell me."

Nikolai smirks, but there's a deadly gleam in his eyes.

"Oh, you're gonna love this one, Boss."

"How so?"

He smirks. "Piotr's got a woman."

"That's not news."

Piotr fucks around; everyone knows that. He always has. There's always been some woman who caught his eye, only to be tossed aside without a second thought the moment he was done with her.

If Nikolai thinks such information is useful, he's losing his touch.

"No," Nikolai says, as if reading my thoughts, "not like that. This one's different."

I wait.

"She's a secret."

Now, that *is* interesting.

"As in, he's hiding her from everyone, even his family?"

Piotr doesn't hide his women. He flaunts them. Parades them around like trophies as proof of his status, his power. The fact that this woman has been kept in the dark, away from prying eyes, means there's something more going on.

"She's not just a random girl he's fucking when he's bored?"

Nikolai shakes his head. "Could be. But if that's the case, why keep her hidden?"

I lean back in my chair, running my tongue over my teeth, considering.

"She must know something."

Nikolai leans forward. "I've been tailing Piotr for some time. That's how I found out about this woman. He only meets with her at expensive hotels throughout the city. They enter separately, leave separately."

I nod, indicating for him to go on.

"I followed her after one of their recent trysts. She treated herself to a little spending spree after they had their fun, bought herself some designer clothes and shoes, a new Chanel handbag."

"So she's a kept woman, not just a fling."

"That's what I'm thinking. Anyway, I approached her when she stopped for a post-shopping cocktail."

"You actually spoke with her?" I can't help but grin at his audacity.

"It took a little bit of smooth talk, but I managed to find out more about her and Piotr's relationship. Nothing specific, just broad details."

"Don't keep me in suspense. Does she know about his business?"

Nikolai nods. "She does. And not just about his current business either. She claims to have information about what happened six years ago."

My stomach tightens. That sounds too convenient.

"Seems odd for her to share that kind of information."

He shrugs. "All I had to do was mention the family name, and her eyes lit up. She tried to play it off, but it was too late. A little prying, a veiled threat, and she was ready to chat."

I take a deep breath, thinking it over.

"You believe her?"

"I believe she knows something," he replies, "whether it's the truth or not is what we need to find out."

I don't like it. The timing is too perfect, too easy. "Is she willing to talk?"

Nikolai nods. "She's willing to talk. But she wants something in return."

I scoff. "Of course, she does." I'm not the least bit surprised. Instead of just doing the right thing without any expectation, people always want something in return, be it money, protection, or power.

One thing I've learned in this role is just how reprehensible people can be. A small amount of money, an empty promise of status, and you can get them to do whatever you want. The number of people who'd sell out everyone they claim to care about for some pocket change is enough to make one more than a little cynical.

"How do we know she won't sell us out the same way?" I question. "This could be a plot spun by Piotr."

Nikolai smirks. "We're her best shot at survival. If Piotr finds out she's been talking, she's dead. I don't think he's got the brains to pull something like this off."

There are far too many unknowns here. Too many what-ifs circling in my head. Finally, I ask the one question I should have asked first. "Does he care about her?"

Nikolai tilts his head, considering. "She was cagey about the details of their relationship."

That doesn't sit right. He's treating her differently than all his other girls, but why? If she doesn't mean anything to him, why keep her hidden? Why make sure no one in his family knows about her?

Something isn't adding up. "She either has something on him," I say, more to myself than to Nikolai, "or she's smart enough to know how dangerous he is."

Nikolai nods. "Or both."

It's a risk. A big one.

I'm still thinking that this could be a trap, a setup, a way to get me chasing my own tail while Piotr plans another move. Or this could be the only way forward. Information is the most valuable weapon in the Bratva. Money hasn't bought the truth. Threats haven't forced it out. But this woman could hold the key.

"Bring her in."

Nikolai smirks, pushing off the edge of my desk like he's been waiting to hear those words. "Figured you'd say that."

I narrow my eyes. He seems too smug, too fucking pleased with himself. "You already set up a meeting, didn't you?"

He shrugs, like it's the most obvious thing in the world. "She's expecting to hear from me. I figured that once you learned all of this, you'd want to move fast."

I let out a slow breath, tamping down my irritation. Nikolai is good at what he does, but sometimes he forgets his place. I give the orders. I make the calls. But I don't tell him he's crossed a line because the truth is, he did good, and I need this information.

"She doesn't want to be tied to Piotr anymore," he continues. "Doesn't want to be part of his world."

I tap a finger against the desk, thinking. Fear can make people reckless, but it also makes them desperate. "So she could have something on him that gives us an edge."

"She could, or she could be talking to Piotr right now."

"You think she'd do that?"

"My opinion? She thought she was getting a ticket to Easy Street, realized she was in way over her head, and now doesn't know how to get out of it."

"And that's where we can offer a lifeline," I say.

Nikolai nods in agreeance.

"If she talks to me, she's protected," I state matter-of-factly.

The weight of that promise settles between us. This is my game now, my rules. If she has legitimate information, it could change everything. If she doesn't, it's back to square one.

Nikolai heads for the door. I watch him go before exhaling a long breath, then dragging a hand over my face. I should be focusing on the bigger picture, on what this woman might know, on what Piotr's next move might be. But instead, my thoughts drift back to Kat, to my wife, to the woman who could very well be my biggest threat. That, or the only thing keeping me safe. She's still the biggest mystery of all.

I have no idea which side she'll choose when the truth becomes clear, but I'm going to find out.

CHAPTER 19

KAT

I wake up starving.

Not just normal morning hunger either. I'm ravenous. A sharp, insistent pang gnaws at my stomach, and the only thing that sounds even remotely satisfying is fried potatoes with onions from Belov's.

I groan, rolling onto my back, staring at the ceiling as my stomach growls in protest. I haven't had cravings like this since... I shake my head, banishing the thought.

This is ridiculous. I can make my own damn potatoes. They won't be the same—nothing ever tastes quite like Belov's buttery, golden-fried perfection—but it'll have to do.

I climb out of bed, stretching as I pad across the room. The penthouse is quiet. It's early, the morning light still soft as it filters through the floor-to-ceiling windows. I don't know why I thought Pavel would still be in bed. He's never in bed when I wake up.

After grabbing a glass of water, I find him in his home office, the door slightly ajar. He's standing near his desk, putting on his cuff links, his suit pristine, tailored, and perfect. An image of power and control. He glances up when he hears me, a slow smirk curving his lips. "You're up early," he says. "Miss me?"

I roll my eyes but can't help the smile tugging at my lips. "Not exactly."

His smirk deepens. "Liar."

He gives me a once-over, and I realize that I'm in nothing but an oversized T-shirt and a pair of panties. Judging by the wolfish look on his face, he's enjoying the view. I cross my arms, leaning against the doorframe. "I'm going to ignore the size of your ego. The truth of the matter is that I woke up starving."

He lifts a brow. "Starving? For what?"

I hesitate for half a second, feeling absurd for even saying it out loud, and sigh dramatically. "Fried potatoes with onions from Belov's."

He chuckles, shaking his head. "That's quite specific."

"I know."

"Want me to have them delivered?"

I blink. That was unexpected, thoughtful. Something a real husband would do. For a second, I almost say yes, but then I shake my head. "No need to spend a hundred dollars having a guy on a bike bring them to me. Though, I appreciate the effort. I can make them myself." Then, tilting my head playfully, I add, "You want me to make extra for you?"

He glances at his watch and sighs. "Tempting, but I have too much shit to deal with today. And I already ate."

Something about the way he says it gives me pause. There's tension in his jaw, a flicker of something unreadable in his expression, like he's trying to hide something. "Everything okay?" I ask.

There's a brief hesitation before he says, "It will be."

He's deflecting. It's not the first time I've noticed; it's been happening often lately. Whatever's going on, it's weighing heavily on him. I open my mouth, about to press the issue, but he smoothly changes the subject.

"What's on your agenda today?"

I hesitate for half a beat, then force a smile. "Thinking about going to see Vlad. Maybe doing a little shopping."

He studies me for a long moment, and I wonder if he knows I'm lying. I shift my weight, watching Pavel as he smooths the front of his suit jacket, looking effortlessly put together, even though I know his mind is miles away, tangled in whatever Bratva disaster he's about to walk into.

Still, when he looks at me, he's focused and present. Like I'm the only thing that matters in the moment.

"That's all you're going to do today?" he asks.

I hesitate. I don't know how much I should tell him. The truth is, I'm going to see Ana, but I'm not ready to share her with him yet. Maybe someday, but not now. All the same, I need to throw him off the trail. For some reason, he seems extra skeptical today.

"That's all," I confirm. "I was planning on keeping it pretty low-key."

"You don't have to keep it low-key if you don't want to."

"What do you mean?"

"Go have a girls' day out. Spend some time with your friends."

I pause, blink in mild confusion, then chuckle lightly, shaking my head. "Friends? I don't really have any."

His brow furrows. "You don't have any? Why not? You used to."

I shrug. "We just drifted apart after high school, I guess. Some went to college, others got married and moved on."

And some had secret babies, then stayed away for six years.

Pavel leans against his desk, arms crossed over his chest as he watches me. "And that doesn't bother you?"

I exhale, considering his words. It never used to. "Not really," I lie. "I have Vlad; we've always been close." My voice trails off as I roll my water glass between my hands, the condensation cool and grounding.

Just then a realization settles in, one I can't ignore.

I don't want Ana to grow up the same way.

I almost voice my thought out loud, right then and there. I nearly slip up, telling him about my best-kept secret. Thankfully, I catch myself at the last moment.

Pavel's expression doesn't change, but his eyes narrow, like he's picking apart my words, and examining the weight of them. I look away, my throat tightening. I can feel Pavel's eyes on me, studying me. I worry that he sees right through my lies, that he knows I'm hiding something. Would I be able to keep the secret if he were to outright ask what was on my mind?

I'm not sure.

He checks his watch. "Shit. I gotta run. Got a meeting to get to."

He comes over to me, taking my hands in his own. His touch soothes me in just the right way.

I look down, unable to meet his eyes. What the hell is wrong with me? I've been able to keep myself together so well these last few weeks. But at that moment, my hands in his, I'm on the verge of breaking.

"You sure you're alright?" he asks.

"Yes."

"And you're sure you don't want me to order you some Belov's?"

That gets a small smile out of me. "I'm sure; there are potatoes and onions here. Might do me some good to cook for myself for once."

He places his hand beneath my chin, tilting it up. I instantly get lost in those eyes, those gorgeous, sparkling blue eyes. The eyes of a killer. Something I too often forget.

"I'll be back soon." He kisses me quickly, then leaves. I listen to his footsteps going down the stairs, the chime of the elevator seconds later. Then just like that, he's gone.

The moment Pavel leaves, I want him back, want my hands in his again. I want him to hold me, to tell me everything is going to be alright. A part of me hates the way I need him, but another part wants to give in every time.

I shove the thoughts aside, the grumbling of my stomach propelling me forward. I make my way to the kitchen and pour myself a cup of tea. Next, I pull a few golden potatoes from the pantry. Grabbing a peeler, I work quickly, stripping them of their rough skins, letting the thin curls fall into the sink. Once they're smooth, I rinse them off, then take my knife and begin dicing them into small cubes, each piece uniform in size.

I grab a large yellow onion from the counter, slicing off the ends before peeling away the papery skin. As soon as I cut into it, the sharp, sweet scent hits me, causing my eyes to water slightly. I halve it, then slice it thin, letting the delicate ribbons fall onto the cutting board.

I then move to the stove, setting a heavy cast-iron skillet over medium heat. I drop a generous pat of butter in the pan. It sizzles instantly when it hits the surface, melting into a golden pool. The moment it begins to foam, I toss in the onions, stirring them gently with a wooden spoon, watching as they turn translucent, their edges beginning to caramelize.

The smell is intoxicating. Warm, rich, and familiar. It takes me back to Belov's, a cozy little Russian restaurant tucked into a quiet corner of the East Village. We used to go there as kids. Vlad, Piotr, and me would be crammed into one of the corner booths, while our parents lingered over tea and conversation with friends and family. It was one of the few places where we weren't expected to sit and be quiet, where we were allowed to just be children. The owners knew us by name, and our father, always generous, let us order whatever we wanted.

For me, it was always the potatoes and onions: crispy on the outside, soft on the inside, perfectly seasoned with salt and black pepper, the onions cooked just right. I'd devour them as soon as they were set in front of me, burning my tongue in my impatience, while Piotr and Vlad stole bites from my dish, laughing as I swatted their hands away. I hadn't been back for years.

Standing here, cooking this meal for myself, the memories cling to me as thickly as the scent of butter and onions filling the kitchen.

Once the onions soften, I add the potatoes, spreading them in an even layer. They hit the hot butter, causing an immediate sizzle that fills the quiet space around me. It's perfect; exactly what I wanted.

I grab a plate, slide a generous serving onto it, then sink into a chair at the kitchen table. My recollection from this morning while lying in bed slams into me again, so vivid and sharp, it almost knocks the air from my lungs.

I was pregnant with Ana the last time I craved this dish. Not just craved—obsessed over it. For weeks, all I wanted was fried potatoes and onions. Morning, noon, and night.

My fork stills, hovering near my lips. My stomach tightens. It's simply a coincidence. It has to be. But my hands are already shaking as I set the fork down. My brain scrambles to do the math. Pavel and I have been married almost five weeks. If I got pregnant the night of our wedding...

Oh, dear God, that's enough time.

A rush of heat surges through me, my heart pounding so fast it makes me lightheaded. I stare down at the plate, my stomach twisting. The food that smelled so heavenly just moments ago now feels impossible to eat.

I press a hand to my abdomen, swallowing hard. I need to be sure. I press my other hand flat against the cool surface of the kitchen table, my breath coming in shallow, uneven waves. If I'm pregnant, I'm carrying Pavel's *second* child. He still doesn't know he has a first.

The thought leaves me dizzy. This marriage—this mess we were thrown into—was never meant to be real. It was a political move, a necessary evil, a means to an end, but now? Now, it's become something else. Something definitely real. And the most terrifying part is that I want it to be.

I trust Pavel more than I ever expected to, more than I probably should. I've been watching him, studying his every move, and everything in my gut tells me the same thing: Pavel Fetisov didn't kill my parents.

Piotr has always been so certain. But he's also always been... Piotr. Controlling. Ruthless. Willing to twist the truth into whatever shape serves him best. But if I let myself believe that about Piotr, what does that mean for everything I've built my life around?

I glance down at my hands, realizing they're shaking. Slowly, I lift my T-shirt and press both of them to my stomach, fingers splayed over the soft skin.

Pavel needs to know the truth about Ana. My chest tightens, the weight of the secret pressing down on me harder than ever. I have to tell him.

And I have to do it soon.

CHAPTER 20

KAT

I wave to Ivan and Dima as I step through the front door of the Andreev house, my spirits lighter than they've been in days. Today, I get to see my little girl. After a quick stop at the pharmacy under the guise of buying tampons, I now know for certain there's another one on the way. Having another baby doesn't scare me. I raised Ana alone. If I have to do it again, I will.

I call for Ana and Camille as I head upstairs, expecting to find them in Ana's bedroom, where they usually have their lessons. The room is empty. Frowning, I move toward Camille's room. Nothing. A flicker of unease ripples through me. I check my calendar, confirming that they don't have an outing planned. Pulling out my phone, I text Camille, waiting for a response as I begin searching the house. After several minutes, still nothing.

I head straight to Vlad's office. He's behind his desk, focused on something on his laptop, but the second I enter, he looks up at me. "Where's Ana?" I ask, trying to keep my voice steady.

Vlad frowns. "Upstairs, with Camille." A chill slides down my spine. "No, she isn't. I can't find either one of them."

He looks confused. "What? Where else would they be?"

I don't bother responding. I turn on my heel, moving quickly through the house. Vlad is right beside me, matching my pace. Piotr's office door looms ahead.

I don't hesitate. I throw the door open, and freeze. Piotr is in there, but he's not alone. A beautiful young woman—half-dressed, flushed, and embarrassed—scrambles to pull on her dress, while Piotr buttons his shirt. He doesn't look the least bit embarrassed. The smell of sex is thick in the air, and it makes me want to retch.

Vlad bursts out laughing. "Well, this is fucking awkward."

I can only stare as the woman fumbles with her clothes, her hands shaking as she yanks her dress over her head. She doesn't even bother with the zipper, too desperate to get away from the situation.

Piotr smirks, running a hand through his hair, completely unbothered. "Do you two ever knock?"

The woman avoids looking at any of us as she bends down, grabbing her shoes from the floor. She turns to Piotr and opens her mouth, ready to say something. But she doesn't get a chance to speak.

Piotr barely glances at her as he buttons his cuffs and says, "Get out."

Her face burns red, but she doesn't argue. She scurries toward the door, head down, heels clutched tightly in her hands.

I step aside to let her pass, my arms crossing over my chest. The second she's gone, I glare at my brother. "You really shouldn't treat women like that. Hell, you shouldn't treat anyone like that."

Piotr laughs as he finishes tucking in his shirt. "Women throw themselves at me. I don't have to treat them like anything. If she doesn't like it, there's a long line of replacements who'd claw each other's eyes out for a chance at her spot."

I scoff. "Right. You know, that's exactly the attitude that gets men stabbed in their sleep, maybe even by their own sisters."

Vlad snickers, but Piotr just smirks. "Sounds like you're speaking from experience."

I take a step forward, my patience wearing thin. "Where. Is. Ana?"

The smirk fades from his face, his expression hardening in mock concern. And just like that, I know. Something is wrong. Piotr moves behind his desk, taking his time before sitting down. His lips curl in amusement, his next words gutting me. "She's not here; neither is Camille."

"Where is she? Tell me now."

"No."

I feel dazed, like I'm in the middle of a bad dream. What the hell is going on?

"No?"

"You won't see her again until you kill Pavel."

My entire world goes black.

Vlad whips his head toward Piotr. "What the fuck?"

Piotr leans back in his chair, completely at ease. "When Pavel's dead, you can have your daughter back."

Rage floods through me. I lunge across the desk. I don't care about the consequences, don't care about anything except ripping him apart. Vlad grabs me, holding me back.

I snarl at Piotr. "You promised me time!"

Piotr shrugs, rolling his eyes as if he's bored. "You've had enough time."

My blood runs cold. "This is kidnapping."

"Perhaps. But who are you going to tell?"

My chest tightens, a mixture of fear and fury taking over. My heart screams at me to do something, to protect my daughter. "If anything happens to Ana, I'll kill you myself," I hiss.

Piotr leans forward. "If you're so willing to kill your own brother, you should have no problem killing your husband."

The smug dismissal in his tone causes something in me to snap. I start screaming as Piotr waves a hand through the air and two men appear. They grab me and drag me toward the door.

I fight—kicking and twisting, punching one in the stomach—but that only causes their grips to tighten. I scream louder, doing all I can to break free of their grasp. Vlad yells at them to let me go. One of them grabs his arm and twists it high behind his back, rendering him helpless. The other one pulls me downstairs and roughly pushes me into the living room. Vlad is right behind us, the other goon shoving him hard.

"You're not to go upstairs," one of them says, "neither of you." Without another word, the guards leave the room. I watch as they take position in front of the staircase, forming an impenetrable wall.

I whirl toward Vlad. A long moment stretches between us, heavy and suffocating. My stomach twists, paranoia sinking its claws into me. I take a step back, my hands trembling. "You knew, didn't you?" I snarl. "You knew Piotr was going to do this."

His eyes widen, his nostrils flaring. "What?"

"You're working with him," I yell, rage and betrayal twisting in my chest. "You—"

Vlad's expression turns to stone, pain shadowing his eyes. "You really think I'd do that?"

I cross my arms, desperate to steady myself. "Piotr took my *daughter*."

"My *niece*," Vlad adds, stepping closer. "How could you think I would help him use her as a fucking pawn?"

I pause, trying to catch my breath, trying to wrap my mind around this new reality.

Vlad shakes his head, exhaling sharply. "You're losing it, Kat. I can understand how desperate you must feel right now, but I would never do that. Never. And you know it."

My throat tightens, my heart aches. He's right. Vlad might be a lot of things, but he isn't anything like Piotr. I inhale slowly, trying to force oxygen into my lungs. "I'm sorry, I just don't know what to think right now."

Vlad nods. "I get it. But I promise you, I had no idea about any of this." He steps forward, gripping my shoulders. "We're going to find her. Together."

I close my eyes, willing myself to believe him. Then I open them, meeting his gaze head-on, and say, "I need to go."

"No, Kat, not in this condition. You shouldn't be alone."

"Don't tell me what I should or shouldn't be," I snap. "I'll be in touch." With that, I grab my keys and storm out before he can say anything else, tears burning my eyes at the thought of my missing girl. But I'll get her back.

No matter what it takes.

CHAPTER 21

KAT

The moment I step outside, the sharp winter air cuts through me, but I barely feel it. My pulse is a constant roar in my ears, my breath coming fast and shallow.

Don't cry. Not here. Not where he can see.

I force myself to keep walking, my heels clicking against the driveway, each step fueled by sheer determination and fear. My hands tremble as I throw my purse into the car and slide into the back seat.

"Home, Mrs. Fetisova?" Ivan asks.

I simply nod, not trusting myself to speak just yet. Piotr has Ana. The words repeat in my head like a horrible chant: *Piotr has Ana. Piotr has Ana. Piotr has Ana.*

He took my child.

Vlad will do everything he can to find her, I know that much. But that might not be enough, not when Piotr is involved. If he's willing to use my daughter as leverage to force me to commit murder, what else is he capable of? When Piotr digs his claws in, he doesn't let go. He now has my daughter in an undisclosed location.

A shuddering breath escapes me as I grip the door. Pavel doesn't know about Ana, and telling him under these circumstances feels wrong. But what other choice do I have? I'm alone in this. I have no power. No moves to make. I blink rapidly, pressing my fingers to my temples, trying to fight the panic rising in my chest.

Breathe. Focus. Think.

The city is a blur as we speed down the streets. I barely register the buildings and lights flashing by. The car turns a corner, things becoming clearer as I spot a woman walking alone. Recognition slams into me: It's the woman from Piotr's office. The one he so carelessly discarded and left scrambling for her clothes. Why the hell is she walking?

Frowning, I glance out the back window. She looks lost. Piotr didn't even bother to get her a ride home. Typical. What a prick. The rage that had only just started to settle flares again for a new reason. "Ivan," I call up front.

"Yes ma'am?"

"We're picking someone up," I tell him, the decision already made.

Silence. Then a heavy sigh. "That's not a good idea."

"We're doing it anyway."

Ivan exhales sharply. "I'm calling it in. Your husband needs to know."

"Fine, but pull over."

Ivan pulls the car to the curb. I lower the window as soon as the woman approaches. "Need a ride?" I ask. She freezes and her eyes widen in surprise, relief flashing across her face. But the relief is quickly tempered with worry when she realizes who I am.

"You're his sister."

"I am. And I can't apologize enough for his behavior. I assure you we were raised better than that."

She bites her lip, glancing away. This young woman, whatever her name might be, is stunning. Sharp, Slavic features, deep green eyes, full lips. Her shape is curvy, ample in all the spots where men like women to be ample.

Finally, she nods, hurrying around to the other side of the car.

"Thank you," she says as she climbs inside, clutching her coat tighter around herself. She looks shaken. I grab a few tissues from the center console and offer them to her.

"I'm sorry my brother's such a dick."

The woman allows herself a laugh, dabbing at her eyes.

"I'm Kat," I offer my hand.

She hesitates but takes it. "Darya."

I watch Darya from the corner of my eye. Her shoulders are curled inward, her hands twisting the now crumpled tissues I gave her. She looks fragile, on the verge of falling apart completely.

She catches me staring and offers a weak smile. "Sorry," she mumbles. "I'm just not used to this."

"Used to what?" I make sure to keep my voice gentle as I speak.

"Kindness."

I hesitate, wondering how to approach her without scaring her off. "Well, I'm sorry to hear that, Darya. So, tell me about yourself. Do you live around here?"

She exhales, staring out the window at the passing buildings. "I'm renting a tiny place with a roommate in Bushwick right now," she says. "I moved to the city a few years ago. I met Piotr at a club one night, and, well, I guess you can figure out the rest."

"Do you work? Go to school?"

"I wait tables," she says quietly, as if ashamed. "Nothing fancy. Just enough to pay the rent and keep up with the bills."

There's a flicker of vulnerability in her eyes, so I don't push too hard. "I'm guessing Piotr didn't tell you much about his business?"

She lets out a bitter laugh. "He makes it clear I'm not supposed to know anything about him. Doesn't want me asking questions, doesn't want me around when he's talking business. Guess he assumed I'd never overhear anything."

"And yet, you did."

She nods once, with her lips pressed tightly together. "And now I'm stuck. I know too much, but not enough to protect myself."

"You're not stuck anymore, Darya. I know you're scared, but I promise; you're safer with me than you were on your own."

"I just...I don't want to be dragged into something bigger than me."

"I get it. But it's already bigger than both of us. Piotr's playing a dangerous game—one that puts people at risk. If you stay out there on your own, you'll be the perfect target."

"I don't know if I can trust you."

"Then trust the fact that we both want the same thing," I say firmly. "To keep Piotr from destroying more lives."

She doesn't respond right away, but finally, she nods, brushing a tear from her cheek. "Alright, I'll try."

It's not a declaration of faith, but it's a start. She seems nice, smart, not the kind of woman I'd expect Piotr to keep around. But she is sleeping with my brother, which means I can't trust her, not entirely. This could all be part of his game.

Still, just because I don't trust her doesn't mean she can't be useful. There's no harm in asking a few questions.

I keep my tone casual. "How long have you and Piotr been seeing each other?"

She sniffles and wipes at her eyes. "A couple of years."

I glance at her, frowning. "A couple of *years*?" I repeat, just to make sure I heard her correctly.

She nods. "Two years, almost. But we're not really together. It's just for fun or, at least, it was. What you saw just now, back at the house, that's not normal."

"I'm confused. You and Piotr haven't been sleeping together?"

Her eyes flash. "No! That's not what I meant. I meant it happening in his office is not normal. Normally, everything we do happens at hotels. We meet, and then he sends me off with a little spending money." She pauses, as if processing her words. "God, it sounds so bad when I put it like that. I don't ask for the money."

"It's fine. No judgment here."

"But you know what the worst part is?"

"What's that?"

She shifts her weight, and I can tell that whatever she's going to say next isn't easy for her.

"I always think that the next time we meet, he's going to want to take things to a more serious place. I know it's stupid, but I can't help it. When he said that he wanted to meet at his house, my heart leaped a bit. He had invited me to stay the night for the first time. Part of me hates him, but another part jumped at it, certain that he was ready to turn this into something more than a two-year-long fling. God, I'm such an idiot."

I laugh. "You're not an idiot, Darya. It happens. When someone has their hooks in you, sometimes they use that leverage to make you dance around a bit."

I'm trying to keep things light, but I'm really pissed. Piotr is notorious for treating women this way. Darya has no idea how many women my brother has pulled the same stunt with over the years. He takes what he wants, when he wants it, but he usually doesn't keep women around for as long as he's kept Darya.

"Sometimes I overhear, but sometimes he tells me things he probably shouldn't."

"Like what?"

Darya immediately stiffens. "It's just pillow talk."

Bullshit.

I press harder. "What do you know, Darya?"

Her hands clench in her lap. "Nothing," she blurts out too quickly.

Liar.

I keep my gaze straight ahead. "If you're scared, we can protect you."

She lets out a hollow laugh. "You can't protect me from Piotr. No one can."

A chill curls around my spine. Darya might not realize it, but she just confirmed something I've suspected for weeks. Piotr isn't just dangerous, he's evil.

We reach an intersection. As Ivan slows the car down, I make a decision before I can second-guess myself. "Come with me."

"Where?"

"To my house."

"Ma'am, I don't—" Ivan protests from the front seat.

She turns to face me, her expression one of confusion. "Why?"

"So you can talk to my husband."

She stills completely.

"Pavel Fetisov."

A ragged breath leaves her lips. "No-o-o."

"Why not?"

Darya swallows hard, her nails digging into her palm. "A man working for him has been trying to contact me. I've spoken to him once. I don't want to get any further into this than I already am."

"I'm afraid it's too late for that. It's best you talk to him."

She shakes her head back and forth several times. "I can't—"

"You don't have a choice."

Darya's breath hitches, a fresh round of tears spilling down her cheeks. She understands that however deep she thought she was in before, she's now in deeper.

And there's no going back.

CHAPTER 22

PAVEL

"Repeat that."

I grip my phone tighter, irritation hot beneath my skin.

Ivan doesn't hesitate. "Your wife had me pick up a strange woman off the street."

I slowly exhale as I press my fingers to my temple, forcing myself to stay calm. What the fuck is she thinking?

"She asked you to stop the car?"

"Yes. They talked for a minute, then the woman got in." Ivan speaks quietly, so that Katerina can't overhear him.

My first instinct is to tell Ivan to turn the damn car around and tell the woman to get out. But I already know that would be useless. Kat doesn't do caution. She follows her gut, consequences be damned. It's one of the things I love about her. She's stubborn, loyal, relentless. She does what she thinks is right, and no one—not me, not her brothers, not an entire fucking Bratva—can stop her.

But right now it's a liability.

"Anything else?" I ask.

"Yeah. The woman came from her brothers' house."

My grip tightens on the phone. That's not a coincidence.

"She was inside?"

"Yeah. Left on foot shortly after Kat showed up."

Before I can ask anything more, my phone buzzes with another call coming in. It's Nikolai.

"Bring them both here," I tell Ivan. "I've got to go. Nikolai's on the other line."

"Understood."

I switch over to Nikolai. "Tell me you have something." I have a feeling I know what he's going to say.

"That woman your wife picked up is the same woman I spoke to earlier."

Just as I'd suspected. "You said he never met her at his house, only at hotels."

"That was the truth, until last night, that is."

"You have this woman's address?"

"Yep, just got it. Some shitty walk-up in Bushwick. I talked to her roommate."

"Go on."

"She didn't seem too concerned." He pauses. "But this time's different, isn't it?"

It's too fucking convenient. Piotr's lover, alone on the street, right after spending the night at his place for the first time. And Kat, of all people, just happens to be the one to pick her up? I don't believe in coincidences. I clench my jaw, my instincts buzzing. "Get to the house—now."

Nikolai doesn't hesitate. "On my way."

I pocket my phone, my mind already three steps ahead. Kat just walked into something, and I'm going to find out exactly what it is.

I settle into my chair, watching the live feed from the security cameras as the car pulls into the garage. Ivan gets out and moves to the back door, opening it for Kat. She moves quickly, exiting the vehicle and walking around to the other side. Kat opens the door for the young woman. She hesitates before stepping out.

I study her. She appears disheveled—messy hair, smudged makeup, like she's been crying. Her clothes are wrinkled, her shoulders slightly hunched. She looks like she's been through hell. I sigh, pushing to my feet. Time to figure out what the hell is going on.

By the time I get to the kitchen, Kat is already there and the woman is standing beside her. I don't give her a chance to speak before closing the distance between us. I cup the back of her neck and press a kiss to her lips. It's brief but firm, a silent claiming. She stiffens for half a second before melting into it.

Satisfied, I pull back, my gaze flicking to the woman, who won't meet my eyes. That's fine. I give her a once-over, wondering what she's thinking. If this woman has dirt on

Piotr, then Kat's impulsive decision might have just given me leverage.

"This is Darya," Kat says by way of an introduction.

Darya finally looks at me, her eyes red-rimmed and wary.

"Pavel Fetisov," I say, extending a hand. She looks at it for a moment like it might be a trap, then cautiously takes it. Her touch is tenuous, like all life has gone out of her. I noticed she'd flinched at my name. Good. She knows exactly who I am. I don't have time for games. I want answers, and I want them now. But, of course, Kat has other plans.

"She needs a minute," she says, giving me a pointed look. "Let her clean up, change into something else."

I exhale through my nose, my jaw clenching. We don't have time for this.

Darya stands awkwardly near the kitchen island, hands gripping the strap of her purse like it's a lifeline. She looks fragile, which is exactly how Kat sees her.

I nod.

Kat looks surprised, like she expected me to argue.

"There's a guest bathroom upstairs," I say. "Spare clothes are in the dresser, there should be some in there that will fit you. Take a shower or a bath, if you need to."

Darya's eyes flash with surprise, as if she hadn't expected such kindness. "Thank you," she says softly.

"But," I say and raise my finger, "leave your phone here."

Without a word, she reaches into her purse and takes out her phone, setting it on the counter.

"This way," Kat says. "I'll show you the room." With that, they leave the kitchen.

As they disappear, I lean against the counter, rubbing a hand over my jaw. I replay everything I know about Piotr in my mind, everything I've suspected. My eyes flick toward the hallway where Darya disappeared. She's curvy, like Kat, like Piotr's mother. My stomach tightens slightly. Coincidence? Maybe, or maybe, it's just one more thing to add to the growing list of what the fuck is wrong with him.

The second Kat steps back into the kitchen, I know this isn't just about Darya. There's tension in her shoulders and a shadow in her expression that wasn't there before. It's subtle, but I know her well enough to see it.

"You okay?"

She hesitates just enough to confirm my suspicion.

Then she says, "After you talk to Darya, we need to chat."

Her words are too controlled, too definitive. I don't like it. Not at all. My muscles tense. "Chat about what?" My tone is sharper than I intend, but I don't like this kind of vague bullshit.

She exhales and crosses her arms as if protecting herself. "Handle her first." She nods toward the hallway. "It'll help with our discussion."

I don't fucking like that either. But before I can press again, Darya reappears. She steps tentatively into the kitchen, her posture stiff, her fingers gripping the hem of the oversized sweater she's changed into. Her hair is damp, her face scrubbed clean. Without the smudged makeup and red-rimmed eyes, she looks younger, prettier but still fragile.

Kat straightens beside me. "I promised her protection."

I glance at my wife before turning to Darya. "If what you know is as valuable as I've heard it is," I begin, eyes locking onto hers, "I'll protect you from the devil himself. Now, let's begin."

CHAPTER 23

PAVEL

"Right this way."

I guide Darya down the corridor toward my office, aware of every hesitant step she takes. She's wearing a borrowed sweater from Kat, her damp hair loose around her shoulders, still looking like she's just been crying.

Under normal circumstances, I'd feel sorry for her. But these are far from normal circumstances, and I'm too on edge, too aware of her connection to Piotr.

I'm torn. Part of me wants to help this young woman, give her some assurance, some peace of mind. Another part of me, however, is all too aware that this could be some sort of trap set by Piotr. I'm not certain she's innocent. Not yet.

My office door stands open, the dim light inside illuminating the dark wood and leather furniture. I gesture for Darya to enter first. She does, but with clear caution. It's as if she's expecting a gang of armed men to be waiting for her, ready to punish her for her betrayal.

I close the door behind us.

"Sit," I say, motioning to the couch near the far wall.

She obeys, perching on the edge of the cushions. Her eyes skitter around the room, never landing on one object too long, like she's searching for an escape route.

I cross to the small bar cart by the window and pour myself a scotch. "You drink?"

"I... yes. Please."

I pour another into a crystal tumbler and hand her the glass, leaning back against the edge of my desk, arms folded across my chest. "Sip slowly; it's strong."

She takes a sip, then another, closing her eyes for a moment, savoring the taste. I can sense the booze is already working its magic, putting her at ease.

"Thank you," she says softly, her gaze flicking up to meet mine for a brief moment before dropping again.

I allow myself to watch her, to gauge her reactions. She's a little pale, eyes swollen from crying, but there is a backbone under there.

"I'll keep you safe," I tell her, "as long as you do your part. I can't protect you without you giving me something in return. By that, I mean information and cooperation. Understand?"

She nods, swallowing hard. "Yes. That's why I'm here. Kat said you could help."

Kat. Always diving head-first into chaos.

"For the moment," I continue, "you can stay here. Or I can set you up in a hotel out of town, someplace no one would think to look."

Darya's mouth forms a flat line. "I don't like either choice. I have a job. I can't just vanish, and I know I don't want to stay here, in this world."

I shrug. "Then handle your own protection. I'm not assigning a bodyguard to follow you around the city," I say coldly.

She frowns, looking toward the door like she's considering running. "You said you'd protect me."

"And I will, but only if you agree to my terms. You can choose from two options: Stay under my roof or let me hide you elsewhere. If you refuse both, it's at your own risk."

She grips the tumbler, knuckles white. "I'll think about it."

"Do that. In the meantime—" I pause as footsteps approach outside, a familiar stride. The door opens, and Nikolai steps inside, flicking a glance at Darya before turning his attention to me.

"You said it was urgent, Boss."

"Indeed." I wave him closer. "Darya, this is Nikolai, my second-in-command. You can speak freely."

She eyes Nikolai warily, then takes another sip of her scotch. "You want to know what I know."

"That's right." My gaze drills into her. "Start from the beginning."

She sets the tumbler on the coffee table, folding her hands in her lap. "I know Piotr hired men to attack those shops a few weeks back. He was bragging about it, proud of how it stirred up so much tension among your people."

I keep my expression neutral, though inside, annoyance flares. If Piotr orchestrated those attacks, it means he's far bolder than I gave him credit for.

"Go on," I quietly urge.

Darya's voice trembles a bit. "I overheard him on the phone. He thought I'd left, but I had to come back in to get my purse. He was in the study, talking, laughing, and saying how the Fetisov Bratva would bleed." She grimaces. "He used the name Viktor, but I didn't hear a last name."

Nikolai looks at me. My jaw tightens. Hearsay and rumors. That's all we have. It's her word against Piotr's. "Anything else?"

She glances away, chewing her lower lip. "I heard him mention a timeline. Something about needing it to look like your operations were failing. That's why the shops were targeted—he wanted to make you look weak."

Nikolai curses under his breath. I drag a hand over my face, anger building within.

"I'm sorry. I don't have recordings or texts. Piotr's careful. He doesn't leave evidence."

Nikolai steps to my side, his arms folded. "Novikov wants the Fetisov Bratva gone. That's no secret. If Piotr's dealing with Viktor—"

I finish the thought. "Then we have a major problem, but we have no evidence aside from Darya's testimony."

Her eyes dart between the two of us, fear evident. "I know it's not enough, but it's the truth."

Nikolai exhales, clearly unimpressed but not dismissing her. "So Piotr's cozying up to an enemy, trying to bring down the Fetisovs from the inside. We can't act on rumors, though."

I catch the slightest flicker of guilt crossing Darya's face, like she knows we need more. "He's been working on it for a while," she says quietly. "He's always said he'd find a way to make your men doubt you, that he'd bleed you dry from the inside."

Her words slice through me, causing a fresh wave of anger to surge. My mind goes to Kat—her loyalty, her unwavering sense of family. She doesn't believe Piotr's an angel by any means, but does she know how evil he actually is? I recall the look in her eyes earlier, the urgency in her voice when she said we needed to talk after I handled things with Darya. What is she about to tell me?

My fists clench at my sides. I trust Kat, but a small part of me still wonders, if push came to shove, she'd pick her brother over me. That doubt coils in my gut, making me feel off-balance.

I turn back to Darya. "So that's it? That's the extent of what you know? He bragged about orchestrating attacks, dropping Viktor's name?"

She nods. "That's all. I'm sorry."

Nikolai casts me a sidelong glance. We're at an impasse. We can't do much with words alone, but this, at least, confirms our suspicions. We needed some kind of lead, and now we have it, flimsy as it may be.

"It's fine. As I said earlier, you can stay here if you want, or I'll set you up in a hotel outside of town. Make your decision soon. In the meantime, you will not be going anywhere without an escort. Understand?"

Darya looks ready to protest, but after taking a look at my face, she nods, swallowing her pride or her fear, maybe both. "Understood."

Nikolai clears his throat. "Want me to take her home, Boss?"

I nod. "Yes, make sure you check her apartment before she goes in, and that no one follows you there. Do not let her go anywhere other than work."

Darya stands, smoothing her clothes, her posture stiff and guarded. "Thank you."

I merely nod in response as I watch her leave my office, Nikolai at her side. He gives me one last look over his shoulder that silently says he'll keep an eye on Darya, ensuring she obeys.

I answer his look with a slight nod, and the door shuts. I take a moment to allow the weight of what I've just heard to settle in. Piotr. The man who's supposed to be Kat's family, the man she could choose to protect if she had to, is conspiring with Viktor Novikov to destroy me.

Kat's an Andreev, through and through, but she's also my wife, in name if nothing else. She's begun trusting me, something I didn't think I'd value as much as I do.

How do I approach her with this? If I tell her Piotr's orchestrating attacks, that he's actively trying to bleed me out, will she believe me or will she run straight to him, demand an explanation, and blow my chance to gather real proof?

I pinch the bridge of my nose, exhaling slowly. Another pang of guilt stabs me when I recall the look in Kat's eyes earlier. She said she needed to talk. Something's clearly weighing on her. Is it about Piotr or something else entirely? Regardless, this isn't how I want to find out where her loyalty lies—forcing a confrontation between her husband and her brother. But if Piotr keeps pushing, such a confrontation is inevitable.

I let my hand drop to my side, glancing around the dimly lit room. The clock on the wall ticks steadily, reminding me time is something I don't have much of. Sooner or later, Piotr will make his move. He's cunning, calculating, and ruthless enough to wage a war in the shadows, turning my allies against me.

I can't let him get that far. But I can't risk alienating Kat, either. Not now, when her trust could be the key to stabilizing this entire mess. If I come at her with accusations about her brother and no solid proof, I could lose her. And if I lose her, I lose the chance of keeping the fragile peace I'm clinging to.

So I'll wait and gather evidence. Let Darya stay under my roof, if that's what she ultimately chooses. If she's telling the truth, her knowledge might help me piece together enough to bring Piotr down. If she's lying, well, I'll handle that when the time comes.

For now, the stage is set for a confrontation that may decide the fate of two Bratvas—and the fate of my marriage, because if Kat has to choose between her brother and me, I need to make sure the truth is undeniable.

I take a few deep breaths before pushing away from the desk. The next move is Piotr's, whether he knows it or not.

And when he makes it, I'll be ready.

CHAPTER 24

KAT

"Come with me."

Darya follows Pavel down the hallway, passing by me without so much as a glance. My heart twists at the sight of her, fragile and scared.

They vanish around the corner. Once they've reached the second floor, I step up a few stairs and hear Pavel say, "We can talk in my office."

I sigh. I know that I should go back to the kitchen and leave them to their conversation, but I can't.

I shouldn't be doing this, I think as I ascend the stairs, making my way toward Pavel's office. I know it's wrong, slipping through the halls like a criminal in my own home, pressing my ear to Pavel's office door. I'm ignoring every polite instinct I have. But the second I saw Darya walking on the street, I felt my stomach knot. I knew she had information.

I can hear their voices on the other side of the door, muffled but distinct.

Screw it.

I press my ear against the door and strain to listen. I catch half a sentence here, a stray word there, longing for more clarity. Damn this door. Darya raises her voice slightly. I can't quite make out every syllable, but I can piece some words together.

"...Piotr...bragging...he said he was *pakhan*...better than his father...helped it along..."

My pulse spikes, blood roaring in my ears, and I freeze. A cold dread coils through my gut. Did Darya just say Piotr helped something along? He was always bragging about being *pakhan* at such a young age...so what is it that he helped along?

My heart pounds so violently, I'm sure they can hear it. I press my palm to my mouth, stifling a cry. Is she implying Piotr killed our parents? No. That can't be. I won't believe it. I can't believe it.

I step back from the door, my mind screaming at me to run in there and demand an explanation. But the rest—my body, my heart, my messy emotional side—refuses. If I confront it now, I'll have to face the possibility that it might be true. I'm not sure I can do that. Not yet, anyway. I need more evidence.

Spinning on my heel, I quietly walk away, nearly tripping over a side table in my frantic rush. The hallway feels too tight, the walls pressing in. By the time I reach the stairs, I'm gasping for air.

I find myself in the kitchen, leaning against the island, my hands braced on the cool granite. My mind spins, replaying Darya's words, searching for a way to interpret them that doesn't lead to the unthinkable.

Piotr is cold and cunning. He's ruthless, manipulative, and about as considerate as a drunk bull in a China shop. But killing our parents? That's a whole other level of evil.

No.

There must be some mistake. Darya's lying, or someone paid her to lie, or she completely misheard.

I squeeze my eyes shut, swallowing back a wave of nausea. The idea of Piotr orchestrating our parents' deaths sits like poison in my veins, spreading dread through every inch of me. The nausea lingers, reminding me of my other secret. I need air. I need time to think.

The front door buzzer jars me out of my spiraling thoughts. It rings through the kitchen's intercom, echoing off the tiled walls. I blink, glancing around. Pavel is still upstairs with Darya.

I walk to the small screen on the wall and press the button. "Yes?" My voice comes out steadier than I feel.

"It's Vlad," the front desk guard says. "He's got a woman and a little girl with him."

CHAPTER 25

KAT

"Yes, please let them in."

My heart soars in an instant, warmth and hope flooding me.

Ana. She's here. Vlad found her. Relief surges through me so powerfully it makes my knees buckle. I was so scared. I've missed her so much.

The dread creeps right back in when I realize what this means. It means she's here, in the same home as her father, who knows nothing about her.

The ding of the private elevator entry announces their arrival. I glance in the direction of the stairs, my hands trembling. The relief that Ana's here briefly overshadows the knowledge that a confrontation is looming. Pavel's going to meet her, and the secret will be out.

I shake my head, trying to push that thought away. My daughter is safe. She's here, and I need her in my arms. Everything else will have to sort itself out.

I hurry to the foyer, pushing aside the swirl of conflicting emotions. The elevator doors open, and Vlad steps in, holding Ana's hand. Camille follows closely, looking relieved but worn.

"Mama!" Ana cries, letting go of Vlad and racing toward me.

I kneel, opening my arms wide, and she collides with me. The scent of her shampoo, the warmth of her small body—it's everything. I hug her so tightly I'm worried I might hurt her, but she just giggles, pressing her face into my neck.

"I missed you, Mama!"

My eyes burn with tears. "I missed you too, baby," I whisper, pressing a kiss to her curls.

Vlad stands there, arms folded, a half-smile on his face. But I can see the tension in his jaw, the questions in his eyes.

Are you okay? Did you find out anything about Piotr's plan?

I swallow, giving him a tight nod. He can tell I'm not fine, but at least he won't press it in front of Ana and Camille.

Ana pulls back just enough to beam up at me, pushing a lock of her curls out of her eyes.

"We went to a hotel! It was so cool, Mama. There was a giant pool inside the building!" She stretches her arms wide as if to show me how enormous it was. "There was a slide, and it went round and round," she starts making twirling gestures with her little hands, laughter bubbling out.

My chest feels tight, torn between happiness at seeing her and fury at Piotr for forcing this entire situation.

"A hotel, huh? That sounds like fun."

Behind Ana, Camille stands politely, carrying a small overnight bag and wearing a serene smile. The picture of elegance as always. She gives me a quick nod of greeting.

"It truly was *charmant*. We turned it into a mini vacation, considering the circumstances." A flicker in her eyes tells me she knows there's more to this than meets the eye.

Ana bounces on her heels. "But I have to do lessons again tomorrow," she complains, wrinkling her nose. "Why can't we stay on vacation forever?"

Before I can answer, Vlad's gaze flicks toward me, his expression shifting from concern to apology. That's when I realize Camille may not have known I wasn't aware of the hotel. She must've assumed I knew about the plan from the start, not realizing that it was all Piotr's doing.

Frustration rises within, but it's not Camille's fault. I know she would never do anything to harm Ana.

"Thank you," I say to her, standing up with Ana's hand still clasped in mine, "for taking care of her. I really appreciate it."

Camille dips her head. "A pleasure, as always. But perhaps next time I'll be more...in the loop, as you Americans say."

You don't know the half of it.

Ana tugs on my hand. "I'm hungry. Can we have lunch?" It's at that moment the grandeur of the penthouse hits her. "Wow...this place is *so big*!"

I rub her gently on the back. "Yes, it is. Of course we can have lunch, baby."

I shoot a look at Vlad, who merely shrugs. There's a heaviness in his eyes that suggests we're about to encounter bigger problems.

"Peanut butter and jelly sandwiches?" Ana asks.

"Sounds perfect."

With that, we head to the kitchen.

Camille clears her throat gently as we walk, offering me a small smile. "She's been asking for you nonstop. I'm glad we could bring her here."

I force a shaky smile in return, running my fingers through Ana's hair. "Me, too."

"Where's Uncle Piotr?" Ana asks.

My throat closes up. He's the last person I want her around right now.

"Um, he's busy."

"Okay," she says simply. She's used to the Andreev men always being busy.

Camille steps closer, placing a hand on Ana's shoulder. "We can come back if this is a bad time."

Camille's picking up on the fact that something is amiss. I'm doing a bad job keeping things close to the chest.

"No," I respond immediately, shaking my head. "No, it's fine."

She frowns slightly, studying me. "You are sure?"

I nod firmly. "Yes. Please, stay."

I glance at Vlad, who's been uncharacteristically silent. He's staring at me, worry etched into his features. We have a lot to discuss, but not in front of Ana.

"Just let me get her settled," I say quietly to him, "then we'll talk."

He nods. "Sure."

A million thoughts assault me at once. The biggest one being that Pavel is going to meet Ana—soon.

I set my daughter up at the kitchen island, rummaging for lunch supplies. Vlad hovers near the door, his arms folded. Camille leans against the counter, eyes flicking among me, Vlad, and Ana, obviously sensing the tension. Finally, Camille engages Ana in conversation, giving Vlad and I cover to talk.

"What's going on?" he asks quietly, after coming over to where I'm standing.

I shake my head, not trusting that all of the emotions I'm feeling won't spill over. "Later," I whisper, hoping he'll understand. "Where were they? How did you find them?"

"It wasn't a hotel. They were at Piotr's condo in Long Island City," he says. "He'd lied, told Camille that they had to stay there for their own safety. Didn't take much effort tracking them down."

It's no small relief. I'd imagined them kidnapped by strangers, locked away somewhere, scared out of their minds.

I begin to fix a quick sandwich for Ana while she chats with Camille about something funny. My heart clenches every time I hear her sweet voice and laughter, unable to bear what might've happened if Vlad hadn't found her. The thought of Piotr using her like a bargaining chip makes me grip the knife a little too tight.

I finish making the sandwich, passing it to Ana and watching her take a big bite, jelly on her lip, chewing happily.

My phone vibrates in my pocket. I pull it out, glancing at the screen. It's a text from Pavel.

Wrapping up. I see we have company?

My pulse races. If I don't tell him now, he'll find out soon enough. He'll walk in and see Ana, his own characteristics on her features, and put the pieces together. I stand beside Ana, brushing crumbs from her chin. Her big eyes gaze at me, trusting and adoring. My throat tightens.

For her sake, I want to trust Pavel. But trusting him means telling him about Ana in the midst of all this chaos, with the possibility that Piotr might have had a hand in killing our parents.

I meet Vlad's gaze. He must see the conflict in my eyes because he takes a step forward, his voice low. "Tell him," he says, "before he finds out in the worst way."

"Stay with her," I reply, tears pricking my eyes. "I'll go find him."

Vlad nods, placing a hand gently on my shoulder. Then he turns to Ana, distracting her with some silly story about her favorite cartoon character.

I take a deep breath, then walk out of the kitchen and up the stairs, straight toward Pavel's office. Each step resonates with the finality of what I'm about to do. My thoughts are all over the place; Darya's revelation about Piotr, the threat to my family, the knowledge that my husband is about to meet his daughter for the first time.

One crisis at a time, I tell myself.

Pavel finding out about Ana is going to change everything. A part of me wonders if it'll be enough to shatter the fragile foundation we've built, if Kat Andreev—no, Kat Fetisova—can withstand another earthquake when she's already been lying to her husband's face for six years.

I don't have the answer, but I have to do this for Ana, for us. I square my shoulders as I make my way to Pavel's office, remembering the conversation I overheard just moments ago. That memory alone nearly stops me, the weight of all these secrets too overwhelming, too crushing. But I can't turn back now. I must do this.

As I approach the door to Pavel's office, it opens and Darya appears, her face pale, the sleeves of her sweater pulled down over her hands. She moves quickly past me without a word, her eyes briefly meeting mine as she hurries by.

Nikolai exits the office next, his long strides quickly catching up to Darya. He nods as he goes by.

I walk into Pavel's office cautiously, unsure of what just happened.

"She said she doesn't want to stay here," Pavel says, a hint of irritation in his tone. "I offered to book her a hotel outside of town. She told me she has a life, that she doesn't want to be in any part of our world. I told her I'd give her a short period of time to think about it before she makes her final decision. Nikolai is taking her home and will keep a close eye on her in the meantime."

I'm dumbfounded. Part of me wants to go talk to her myself, remind her how dangerous this is, but another part can't find the words. My entire world is spinning too fast right now. "So, we're just going to let her leave?" I ask, exasperation in my voice.

"What else can we do? I'm not going to kidnap her. I can't force her to stay here. I made it clear that if she doesn't, the promise of protection is off the table. It's her choice; she has all the information she needs to make the right one."

Before I have a chance to say anything else, he changes the subject. "We have guests. I saw them on the security feed. Who is the woman and the girl accompanying Vlad?"

Shit. No getting out of it now.

"The woman's name is Camille, and...actually, let's go to the kitchen to talk."

A flicker of irritation appears on his face. Pavel isn't the sort of man whom you keep information from. But then his expression softens, as if he can sense there's something serious at play.

"Okay," he concedes. "Let's go to the kitchen."

We descend the stairs in silence. When we enter the kitchen, Pavel's gaze lands on Vlad first, then Camille, and finally Ana. She tilts her head, blinking up at him. He takes a step closer, his expression softening into something tender and warm. He looks at her like he's trying to solve a puzzle.

His lips turn upward into the brightest smile as he asks, "And who is this lovely young lady?"

CHAPTER 26

PAVEL

I crouch down in front of the little girl, so we're eye to eye.

She's maybe five, with dark curls, bright eyes, and a timid smile that doesn't quite hide the curiosity dancing beyond it. Kat stands protectively behind her, clearly on edge.

"Pavel, this is Ana," Kat says, a slight tremble to her voice. She looks at the child, then back at me. "Ana, say hello to Mr. Fetisov."

Ana stands up tall before offering a practiced polite bow, her curls bouncing. "Hello, Mr. Fetisov." Her tone is soft but confident. She's obviously been taught good manners.

"Nice to meet you, Ana." I hold out my hand, and she gives it a careful shake with a stern, grown-up expression that almost makes me laugh. Then she giggles, disarming me in an instant.

I stand up, my eyes landing on Vlad. He stands a few feet away, arms crossed, carefully watching the girl. Behind him is a tall, poised woman who I can only assume is Camille, the person Kat mentioned before we left my office to come to the kitchen.

Kat's body language is tense, guarded—shoulders tight, chin raised, eyes scanning the room. Even Ana, who was cheerful just a moment ago, seems to pick up on the tension.

"I am Camille," the woman says with a French accent. She walks toward me and offers her hand. I take it. As we shake, her eyes look me over. She's not checking me out—she's *assessing* me.

What the hell is going on? No one is offering an explanation. It's as if they're waiting for me to piece it together on my own. I feel a strange sensation in my core. A newfound sense of overwhelming purpose. I clear my throat. "Welcome to my home," I say. My voice is low, more subdued than usual. "I'm pleased you could come."

Vlad gives me a polite nod. "Thank you, Pavel. We appreciate it."

Camille smiles politely. "Ana's been asking to see Kat for ages."

Kat exhales sharply, a look of concern and mild shock taking over her expression.

"*Desolee* if we are intruding," Camille says politely.

"Not at all. Come, let's get everyone a little something to eat."

Ana looks up at Kat again. "Mama, I am still hungry."

Mama?

That single word crashes into my thoughts like a bulldozer. Kat is her mother. My mind reels. How? When? Why didn't she tell me she had a child? I can't stop the barrage of questions hammering around inside my skull.

Kat lowers herself to Ana's level, smoothing a stray curl away from the little girl's face.

"Okay, sweetheart. But first, I need to speak to Mr. Fetisov." She gives me a look that begs me not to push. Then she kisses Ana's cheek. "Go with Uncle Vlad and Camille, okay?"

Ana nods, "All right." Then she looks at me again, uncertain. "Nice to meet you."

Camille reaches for Ana's hand, and they head toward the living room. Vlad follows. Kat watches them go before turning back to me, her expression shadowed with anxiety. Her stare pins me in place, silently pleading: *Don't ask, not yet.* I clench my jaw, keeping my questions to myself—for now.

I lead her down a corridor off the kitchen to the downstairs study. We step inside, and I close the door, leaning against it, my arms folded. My mind is a storm of questions, but I wait for her to speak first.

"Thank you," she says quietly.

"For what?"

A tremor passes through her. "For not demanding an explanation in front of everyone, in front of Ana."

I watch her carefully. She's trembling slightly, but anger still lingers in my chest, preventing me from going to her. "Kat, who is that little girl?"

I don't really need to ask, I already know.

She chews her lip, looking away briefly before meeting my eyes. "Her name is Ana, and she's our daughter."

The words are deafening, though I hear them clearly.

"She's our daughter?"

Kat's eyes brim with tears. She nods once. "Yes, she's five. I found out I was pregnant right after my parents died. Piotr sent me away to live with an aunt to keep the baby and me safe."

I see red for a moment, furious at having missed the first five years of my child's life. I clench my fists. "How could you keep this from me?" My words come out sharper than I intend, but I can't help it. The anger is raw, undercut by heartbreak. "Especially after being in my home all this time?"

She flinches, tears threatening to fall. "I'm sorry. At first, I truly thought I was protecting her from you and your family. Piotr had me convinced that you were a danger to us. But now, I don't know what to believe. I just know that I can't live without seeing her every day."

I grit my teeth to hold back a string of curses. Anger, confusion, and a fierce protectiveness surge within me all at once.

"You raised her alone?"

Kat's lower lip trembles. "She's amazing—bright, curious. Vlad and Camille helped. They still do. But I had to be cautious, especially once Piotr started making moves."

A flash of rage and betrayal crosses her face.

I push off the chair, pacing the small space. "Why bring her here now?"

Her eyes turn dark. "Because Piotr took her. He threatened me with her safety unless I..." She exhales before speaking again. "He said I had to kill you, or I'd never see her again."

My blood turns cold, every protective instinct on overdrive. "He used our daughter against you?"

Kat grabs my arm, her eyes wide. "We have to be smart. Piotr crossed a line. If we move impulsively, we risk everything."

She's right. I can't barrel into a confrontation without a plan. "He'll pay," I say firmly. "I won't let him get away with this."

She sighs. "I know."

My thoughts are still spinning as the realization of Ana settles deeper. "My child."

Kat lowers her gaze. "I'm not sorry I protected her, but I am sorry I didn't tell you once I began to suspect Piotr."

"What's done is done. She's here now." A rough laugh slips out, half disbelief, half joy. "I'm furious, but I'm also happy. I have a *daughter*."

Kat's tears finally spill. "Thank you," she whispers, stepping into my arms. I hold her, letting our moment of closeness smooth over my frayed nerves. When we break apart, I feel calmer.

"What now? I won't let Piotr near her."

She stiffens. "We must ensure her safety, then we'll handle everything else—Piotr, the truth about my parents, whatever Darya told you."

"Agreed. She's waiting for us."

Kat musters a weak smile. "Yes. Let's go."

I lace my fingers through hers, leading her out of the study. My mind still spins with the enormity of what we just discussed, but I push it all back. I have a daughter. She's here, in my home. Protecting her comes before everything else.

As we approach the kitchen, we find Ana perched on a stool at the island, kicking her legs and chatting with Camille, who's smiling at something the girl said. Vlad stands guard in his typical stance, arms folded, an odd mix of tension and relief in his eyes.

Camille and Ana turn as we approach, curiosity on their faces. I let go of Kat's hand and step toward Ana. She gives me a shy smile that fills my chest with unexpected warmth.

"You still hungry?" I ask.

She nods; her eyes bright. "Yes!"

A grin twitches at my lips. "Then let's whip you up a snack."

Kat slips in beside me, her presence steady despite her anxiety. We may face threats, we may have to confront Piotr, and we definitely have a million questions to untangle. But at this moment, I soak in the sweet excitement on Ana's face, letting it anchor me.

CHAPTER 27

PAVEL

"Voilà," Camille says with a small smile. "Quiche Lorraine. Simple, but delicious."

She insisted on cooking, and I luckily had all the ingredients already on hand. With practiced ease, she sets the quiche on the table, the golden crust perfectly crisp, the scent of melted cheese, eggs, and smoked ham filling the room.

Ana beams as Camille puts a plate in front of her. "Thank you!" She glances over at me, her feet kicking under the table. "Mr. Fetisov, do you like quiche?"

I smile at the formality. "I suppose we're about to find out."

Camille serves the rest of us, and soon, everyone is happily eating. The room hums with quiet satisfaction, forks tapping against plates.

Ana takes a big bite, eyes widening as she dramatically says, "*Mmm*, it's so good!"

Vlad chuckles. "That's high praise."

Kat shifts beside me, her fingers lightly tracing the rim of her glass. She's watching me closely, gauging my reaction to Ana and the sudden family dynamic settling around us. I know she's bracing for me to snap, to push back against the disruption, but I don't have any intention of doing so.

I glance at Ana, swinging her legs again as she eats. Every so often, she sneaks a peek my way, like she's still trying to figure me out. The weight of it settles deep in my chest. She has no idea who I am to her, not yet. But she's here, in my home, and that's a start.

"So, Ana, what do you like to do for fun?" I ask.

She lights up. "I love to draw, and I used to take dance lessons." She leans in conspiratorially. "But I stopped because the teacher was mean."

Vlad snorts a laugh. "She wasn't mean; she just had rules."

"She yelled a lot," Ana argues.

"Ballet is strict," Camille chimes in, a teasing note in her voice. "But I do recall that teacher being a bit intense."

"See? Camille says the same as me!"

I chuckle. "Do you like books?"

Ana nods her head enthusiastically. "I do!"

"What kind of books do you like?"

Ana considers this, nibbling on a bite of quiche. "Princess stories," she decides, "but not the boring ones. I like the kind where the princess fights the bad guys."

Kat grins. "My brave, strong girl."

Ana smiles at her mother before turning back to me. "Do you like stories, Mr. Fetisov?"

I tap my fork against my plate, pretending to think it over. "I do. But I don't think I've read any princess stories."

Appalled, Ana gasps. "None?"

I shake my head. "Not a single one."

She looks at me like I'm a lost cause, and sighs. "We have to do something about that."

Kat bites back a laugh, and I glance at her before returning my attention to my little girl. "All right, then. You'll have to pick a good one for me."

Ana claps her hands. "I already know which one!"

I smile at her, something unfamiliar spreading through my chest. "It's a deal."

Across the table, Vlad watches the exchange quietly. He doesn't say anything, but there's approval in his eyes.

Kat reaches for her glass again, exhaling softly, the tension fading bit by bit. She looks at me, and I know what she's thinking: This is going better than she expected.

Vlad clears his throat. "Thanks for letting us stay for lunch, Pavel," he says. "I appreciate the hospitality."

I give a curt nod. "Happy to do it. It's about time we shared a meal—all of us."

His gaze slides to Kat, then back to his plate. "Yes, it is."

After that, we fall into easy conversation.

Eventually, I find myself with an empty plate, feeling more relaxed than I have in days. However, my stomach churns slightly with anticipation. Once we finish lunch, I'll have to talk with Vlad and Kat about everything I've learned about Darya's revelations and the looming threats. But for now, I will enjoy the moment with my daughter.

She's quite the chatterbox, describing the water slide at the condo in complete detail. "It went round and round and round," she says, twirling her fork in the air, "then splash! You land in the pool at the bottom. Mama, can we get a pool and a slide like that?"

Kat laughs, a genuine laugh that I haven't heard in a while. "We have a pool, baby, but it's outside, so it's too cold to swim right now."

"Maybe in the summer," I say, giving Ana a grin.

She lights up. "Really? Can we invite Camille?"

"Of course," Kat agrees, looking to Camille for confirmation.

Camille offers a warm smile. "I'd be delighted."

Ana giggles, turning back to her plate. "Yay!" She leans in, whispering loud enough for half the table to hear. "Mr. Fetisov, do you like to swim? I do. I'm a good swimmer. I took lessons!"

I chuckle. "I'm pretty good, yes."

She seems satisfied, resuming her meal. I can't help but notice how comfortable she's become around me in such a short time. It's surreal and oddly wonderful.

The conversation drifts. Vlad cracks a subtle joke about the cartoon Ana forced him to watch five times in a row. Camille tells us how she and Ana tried to feed the ducks in Central Park, only to have the birds chase after them.

Kat's leg keeps bouncing under the table, even as she happily engages with everyone. She's anxious—she knows what's about to happen after we finish lunch. She also likely wonders if I'm still upset with her. I can sense her looking my way every few minutes, gauging my mood.

Camille moves around the table once everyone's finished eating, gathering plates with smooth efficiency. "I'll clean up," she says. "You all talk."

Ana stretches her arms overhead, then pats her belly. "I'm full. That was *so* good! Thank you, Camille."

Camille smiles warmly at Ana as she stacks dishes. "You're very welcome, *petite étoile*. I'm glad you liked it."

Kat catches my eye. "That was lovely. Thank you, Pavel. And Camille, *merci* for cooking."

Camille nods, still clearing. "It was my pleasure, *comme toujours*."

Ana glances between us, suddenly wary. "Mama, you're not leaving me again, are you?"

Kat reaches over, covering Ana's small hand with her own. "Just for a little bit, sweetheart. But I have a surprise for you first."

Ana tilts her head. "A surprise?" Her voice is cautious but hopeful.

I clear my throat, choosing my words carefully. "We're going to prepare a room for you upstairs," I tell Ana, watching her reaction closely. "A space just for you—with toys, a princess bed, and anything else you want or need."

Ana's brow furrows. "But we already live with Uncle Piotr and Uncle Vlad."

Anger coils in my gut at the mere mention of that prick Piotr, but I keep my tone calm and even. "Your mama lives here now. If you want to stay with her, this can be your home, too, but only if you want it to be."

Ana's face shifts from confusion to curiosity, then finally excitement. "Can I see it?"

Kat smiles. "It's not ready yet, but we'll get it set up for you right away."

Ana wiggles in her chair, excitement beginning to outweigh any lingering hesitation. "Can I have lots of pillows and books?"

"As many as you want," I assure her.

She leans forward, lowering her voice. "And toys?"

I smirk. "Obviously."

She grins, the hesitation in her small frame finally easing. "Yay! I want to stay here with Mama."

Relief rushes through me, but I keep my expression neutral. "Good. We will also prepare a room for Camille right next door."

Camille, still at the sink rinsing dishes, turns in surprise. "Oh, my. Well, that's very kind of you, Mr. Fetisov. *Merci beaucoup.*"

Kat nods and smiles. "We'll discuss the details later, but we'd love for you to stay on."

Camille smiles broadly. "I'd be happy to. It's been a while since I've taught in a new place." She looks over to Vlad, who's been quietly listening. "We'll need to arrange to get our things from the house."

Vlad straightens slightly. "I can help with that."

Camille gives him a small nod, something unspoken passing between them.

Kat turns back to me. "Is that alright?"

I rest my forearms on the table, glancing at Ana's eager face, then at Kat's expectant one. "Of course," I reply. "We'll make it happen."

Ana lets out a delighted squeal. "Yay! Can I see my room now?"

Kat laughs, pushing her chair back. "Come on, let's go take a look and start planning."

Ana slides off her chair and grabs Kat's hand, practically bouncing with excitement. "Can I have twinkly lights?" She directs the question toward me.

I realize she's asking my permission, or at least my agreement. It's a strange sensation being consulted about such things, like we're forming a real family dynamic.

"Absolutely," I say. "Whatever you want, within reason, of course."

"Cool!"

"Give them the two guest rooms on the second floor," I say to Kat. "Give Camille the one with the ensuite."

Ana nods eagerly, tugging at Camille's shirt sleeve. "C'mon, let's go see our new rooms!" Camille turns off the water and dries her hands, while Ana practically drags her toward the door.

"I need to talk to you and Vlad," I tell her. "Tell him to join me in my office. You can meet us once Ana and Camille are settled."

She nods. "Alright. She's going to have a million questions." A small smile tugs at her lips. "She always does."

"She's sharp. I'm really glad that I get to be a part of this."

Kat's eyes soften. She reaches across the table and squeezes my hand. "So am I."

I sit for a long moment after she leaves, listening to the faint echoes of Ana's excited chatter upstairs. *My daughter.* The weight of the words settles over me, foreign yet grounding. A fierce, unfamiliar kind of protectiveness grips my chest—something I've only felt for Kat before.

I won't let anyone hurt them, no matter who it is or what it takes. I shove the thought down, keeping it close to the surface.

There's work to be done.

CHAPTER 28

KAT

Ana bounces up the stairs, her excitement barely contained as she reaches the second floor.

"Which one is mine?" she asks impatiently.

I gesture down the hallway. "Come see."

She grabs Camille's hand again and practically drags her along, her little legs working double time trying to keep up with Camille's long strides. When we reach the room Pavel suggested, I push open the door, stepping aside so she can take it all in.

The moment Ana sees it, she gasps. "Whoa."

The space is airy and bright, the large windows allowing natural light to pour in. The view is amazing, the towers of Midtown peeking up from behind the city in the distance.

Ana beelines for the windows. "I can see everything!"

Camille chuckles, resting a hand on Ana's shoulder. "It is quite a view."

"We'll have it decorated however you want. And Uncle Vlad is going to make sure all your toys and things are brought here later today. Do you like it?"

Ana spins around, a big, beaming smile taking up her entire face. "I love it." She hops onto the bed, bouncing once before flopping onto her back with a satisfied sigh. "It's so comfy."

I laugh. "Good, because you're going to be spending a lot of time here."

She shoots up onto her elbows, suddenly serious. "Do I really get to stay here forever?"

My breath catches. There's so much she doesn't know, so much we haven't told her yet. "For as long as you want, sweetheart."

That seems to be enough for now.

Camille watches her fondly before giving me a knowing look. "You did well."

I exhale, relieved. "I hope so." I nod toward the hallway. "Come on, let's go see your room."

Camille follows me to the room next door. I take in her reaction carefully as she surveys the space. The moment she spots the reading nook—a cozy alcove with built-in shelves and a deep window seat—her eyes light up. "This is…" she trails off, stepping farther inside. "It's lovely."

"You like it?"

She runs her fingers along the shelves before turning toward the ensuite. The moment she peeks inside, I hear her gasp. "That tub," she muses. "I might never leave."

I smirk. "That was the idea."

Camille turns to me, appreciation softening her usually composed features. "Thank you, Kat, truly."

I give her a warm hug. She deserves it. "You've taken care of Ana for a long time. It's the least we can do."

She returns the embrace. "I'll make sure she settles in."

We head back to Ana's room. "I need to meet with Pavel and Vlad. Stay close?"

Camille nods. "Of course."

I slip out into the hallway, my thoughts tangled. My daughter is finally safe and home with me where she belongs, but the weight of everything else going on crashes down the moment I step outside that little cocoon.

I pause at the top of the stairs, my hand tightening on the railing. I should have told Pavel about Ana sooner. I almost did more than once. But now we have another baby on the way. Springing two children on him in one day feels like too much.

Ana's arrival alone has turned his world upside down. Adding another layer right now could push him over the edge, but is there ever going to be a perfect time to tell him about the baby?

I take a deep breath, exhaling slowly, shaking off the hesitation. One problem at a time. Right now, I have to focus on what's in front of me. If what Darya said is true—if Piotr orchestrated not only the Bratva war but also our parents' deaths—then we're facing something far worse than I ever imagined.

I make my way down the hall. The door to Pavel's office is slightly ajar, and I can hear the low murmur of voices inside. He and Vlad are already talking. With a quick breath, I raise my hand and knock before pushing the door open.

Inside, the room is bathed in the golden glow of the lamp on Pavel's desk. He stands near the window, a glass of whiskey in his hand. Vlad leans against a bookshelf, his own drink loosely in his grasp. Both men turn as I enter.

"Kat," Pavel says, setting his glass down. "We were just about to call you."

Vlad lifts his drink in a half-salute. "Hey, sis."

I clear my throat. "Sorry for taking so long. I just wanted to make sure Ana and Camille were settled."

"How are they?" Vlad asks.

"Good, I think," I reply, "considering they were both moved across the city without any notice."

The corner of Pavel's mouth lifts slightly. "She's a good kid," he says, almost to himself. "I'm glad she's here, where she's safe." His jaw twitches, darkness shadowing his features, and I know he's thinking of Piotr's involvement.

"I am, too," I step farther into the room. "So, I guess it's time to talk."

Pavel gestures for me to sit. "Would you like a drink?" he asks.

"No, thanks," I say. "My stomach's in knots."

Between the worry over Piotr, the baby I haven't told him about, and the swirl of guilt about how this day went down, alcohol is not an option.

Vlad raises an eyebrow. "You're passing on whiskey?" He tries for a teasing tone, but it falls flat. He knows me well enough to register something's off. I'm not known to refuse a glass of bourbon.

I force a half-smile. "I'd just rather be clearheaded right now."

Pavel nods, swirling the amber liquid in his tumbler. "Alright then. Let's get to it."

I claim one of the armchairs while Vlad remains standing. There's an unease in the air, and I'm eager to get the conversation started.

"Vlad," Pavel begins, "you and I have always gotten along. Even when Kat and I parted ways years ago, you never treated me like an enemy."

Vlad nods his head slowly, acknowledging the statement. "I always believed you were decent, despite what Piotr said."

Something about that sentence rattles me. *Despite what Piotr said.* He's been poisoning the well for a long time.

Pavel continues. "I'm going to tell you something you're not going to like." He spares me a glance, and I know exactly what he means. He's about to disclose the conversation with Darya and what she revealed about Piotr.

Vlad straightens. "If this is about the attacks, I'm already on board. I know Piotr arranged them. Darya might have confirmed it, but we've had suspicions for a while. The men targeted were in smaller shops in Fetisov territory, not Andreev. It was meant to create discord, to weaken your influence."

"So you believe that part," Pavel says, a bit surprised.

Vlad nods grimly. "Yes. Piotr's never hidden his desire to expand. He wants to push you out. I've had my doubts about whether he'd go as far as staging attacks, but I'm not surprised."

I exhale a sigh of relief.

Then Vlad's gaze shifts to me. "Kat, you must have suspected something. Why else sneak around to find information? You brought Darya here, after all."

I purse my lips. "I suspect Piotr is capable of a lot more, of things we don't know about," I say, choosing my words carefully. "He used Ana as leverage against me, so there's no question he's willing to cross lines. But what Darya said was..." I let my words trail off, glancing at Pavel for help.

He picks up the thread. "She implied Piotr might have had a hand in your parents' deaths."

Vlad recoils, disgust taking over his expression. "That's bullshit."

The abruptness of his response is like a punch to my stomach. He's never accepted that Piotr could be involved. He's always tried to see the best in him—even after everything he's done.

"It's what she overheard," Pavel clarifies. "He was bragging about how young he was when he became *pakhan*, how he 'helped it along,' insinuating your father's death wasn't just an accident. That's all we know."

Vlad looks at me as if asking me to refute what Pavel just said. I purse my lips and give him a pleading look, watching the light nearly go out in my brother's eyes.

Pavel rakes a hand through his hair. "I never believed your father's accident was random, but we've always suspected outside involvement. The Novikov Bratva or some other group that wanted to break the alliance, never Piotr."

Vlad shakes his head vehemently. "You're telling me my own brother killed the man who raised him? Our father? That's..." His voice breaks for a second. "That's insane."

I lean forward; my hands clasped tightly in my lap. "Vlad, you know he's changed. We all know. He's not the boy we grew up with who cared about alliances and bridging our families. He's a different person now. He has been for a long time."

Vlad presses his lips into a thin line. "It's one thing to orchestrate attacks in order to push you out of power. But to murder our parents? That's monstrous."

"Exactly," I say. "And that's why I don't want to believe it either. But with what we know, it is possible."

"We have no proof other than Darya's word," Pavel says. "And it sounds like she's not even sure what she heard. But just think about it for a minute. If he is working with Viktor Novikov or some other faction that wants to see us both weakened, it's not that big of a stretch to doing something as extreme as removing your father from power."

Vlad's face contorts with anger. "He's convinced your father or someone in your family had a hand in it. That's been his story for years."

"I loved your parents, Vlad. They were like a second family to me. I'd never—" He clenches his jaw. "You know me better than that."

Vlad exhales sharply, running his hand over his face. "I do, but Piotr doesn't, or at least he pretends he doesn't. He's been on a warpath about the Fetisovs' guilt forever."

"He's the one who told me your family killed my parents, which gave me all kinds of reasons not to trust you. For a while, I believed him," I quietly admit.

Pavel turns to me slowly. "But now you know better."

I swallow hard. "I do."

Vlad sighs heavily, setting his whiskey down on the nearest shelf. "What exactly are you asking me to do here? Accept that my brother could have murdered my parents?"

Pavel takes a deep breath before speaking. "No, not just accept it. We want you to look into it. Discreetly. See if you can uncover anything. If we confront him outright with no evidence, he'll just spin it. But if we have something tangible..."

Vlad clenches his hands into fists at his sides. "That would make him a traitor and guilty of patricide, the worst kind of scum."

"I'm sorry," I whisper. "I don't want it to be true either. But we have to face the possibility."

He stares at me, eyes burning with fury. "Darya said all of this?"

Pavel nods. "Yes. She was here. She refused my protection and left. We can't force her to confirm or clarify anything further, that's if she even lives much longer. Piotr will be after her soon, I would imagine."

Vlad rakes a hand through his hair again, staring out the window. "Fine. I'll go home. I'll watch him, ask nondescript questions. I'll tread carefully. But if he did kill our parents..."

I stand and approach my brother, placing a hand on his arm. "Be careful. He's already used Ana to threaten me. Who knows what he'll do if he suspects you're snooping around."

He looks at me with haunted eyes. "I will." Then he turns to Pavel, extending a hand. Pavel takes it, the handshake is brief but firm.

"Keep me informed," Pavel says quietly.

Vlad nods. "Of course."

Before he leaves, he brushes a kiss against my cheek. "I don't know where this is headed, Kat," he whispers, "but I'll protect you and Ana, no matter what."

Tears sting my eyes. "Thank you."

He offers me a tight, sad smile, then slips out the door. The air instantly feels cold in his absence.

I feel helpless. The possibility that my own brother murdered our parents, that he's a traitor to our family and the Bratva, and that we're standing on the precipice of a war with him, is all too much to bear.

Ana is safe for now, but at what cost? We've escalated the conflict by taking her away. He'll be furious when he finds out she's living with us. A warm hand settles on my shoulder. I turn, blinking back tears. Pavel is looking at me with warm concern in his eyes.

"Kat," he says, and that's all it takes for my composure to shatter.

A sob escapes before I can choke it back. I hate how vulnerable I feel. "I'm sorry," I manage, my voice quivering, "for all of this."

He pulls me into a tight hug. It's warm and solid, and right now, it's exactly what I need.

CHAPTER 29

KAT

I linger in the doorway of our bedroom, my pulse ticking a little too fast.

Dinner was peaceful. The house is easing into its new rhythm effortlessly. Ana is settled in her room with Camille right next door. It was so good to be able to tuck my daughter in again. It's been way too long, and I hadn't realized just how much I'd missed it.

Vlad's gone for the night, making arrangements to have our things sent over. I worry for him, worry what might happen if Piotr were to find out his own family is investigating him.

Pavel stands in front of me, rolling up his sleeves, a small smirk tugging at his lips. "You look tired," he says.

I step into the room. "It's been a long day."

He arches a brow. "That's an understatement."

"You're telling me." I stop mid-step, raising a hand to my mouth. "God, how selfish of me. You found out you're a father today, and here I am, making it all about myself."

Pavel looks away for a moment, then places his hands on my upper arms. His touch soothes me instantly, as it always does. "It's not about you or me. It's about all of us. But especially that little girl down the hall. *Our* little girl."

I smile. My Ana. Just thinking about her has a way of calming me, centering me.

He grins. "I have an idea."

"An idea?"

"Yep. I think a bath might help, hot, with lots of bubbles."

I can't help but laugh. "That does sound good."

"Come with me."

He leads me to our bathroom, flipping on the lights, then dimming them. The tub is massive and inviting. It's also something I unfortunately never seem to have time for. Pavel crouches down and turns on the water, testing it under his hand and adjusting the knobs until he's satisfied. A handful of bath salts, a generous pour of bubble solution, and soon foam is swirling across the surface, a lovely scent of lavender filling the air.

Neither of us says much as the tub fills. We just stand side by side, the sound of running water echoing around us as steam fills the room. My nerves hum beneath my skin, tangled up with exhaustion and anxiety. I should tell him about the baby, but I don't want to break the spell of the moment, not yet.

Pavel tests the water again. "Perfect." He dries his hand off on his pants leg, then asks, "You ready?"

"For a hot, relaxing bath? Always."

His lips twitch, a low chuckle escaping as he pulls his shirt over his head. My breath catches when I look at him. He's all sharp lines and hard muscle. No matter how many times I see him shirtless, it always gets my heart beating faster.

I pull off my own shirt, then reach for my pants. Pavel closes the space between us, his hands finding my waist, his lips softly brushing against mine. He murmurs against my mouth. "You've been keeping secrets, Kat."

The husky warmth in his voice sends heat curling low in my belly at the same time, causing my nerves to jump. Does he know I'm pregnant?

"First Ana," he says, his fingers tracing slow circles against my skin. "Who knows what else you could be hiding?"

I swallow hard, forcing a sly smirk. "I don't know. I guess you'll just have to wait to find out."

He slides his hands down, unbuttoning my pants and tugging them along with my panties over my hips until they drop to the floor. For a second, we just stand there, breathing in the hot, scented air, the sexual tension between us pulsing. All the anger, longing, and secrets boil down into one raw, electric moment.

Pavel unhooks my bra smoothly in one motion, letting it fall away to the floor. The way he stares at my breasts sends a flush of heat through me.

"God, you look good," he mutters.

"You're not exactly hard on the eyes either."

He smirks before taking his pants off, revealing the v-cut of his hips and the thick length of his cock, already hard for me. My mouth waters, desire washing away every other worry. He steps into the tub, then turns to face me. He reaches out a hand, inviting me in, and I take it, sinking into the heated water with him.

I settle between his legs, my back against his chest, bubbles foaming up around us. Instantly, all of the tension in my muscles releases. His strong arms slide around my waist, pulling me close. I can feel his hardness pressing against my lower back.

He leans down, brushing a few kisses along my shoulder while working his thumbs into the knots around my neck. I let out a loud sigh, my head tilting back against him.

"You did great today," he murmurs against my skin. "Ana's amazing."

I bite my lip, nodding. "She really is. I'm so sorry you missed those years with her."

He exhales; his breath hot against my neck. "I'm not letting that overshadow the fact that I have her here now," he says. His hand slips beneath the water, caressing my belly. "And there's a lot more at stake."

A lump of guilt builds in my throat. I can't keep this secret forever; it's only right he knows. But his arms feel so good around me, the hot water soothing all of my anxiety away, and selfishly, I just want to savor it.

Steam swirls around us as he kisses below my ear, sending a wave of warmth straight through me.

"I'm proud of you," he whispers. "For raising her so well, for everything."

My fingers graze his thigh beneath the bubbles, feeling the tautness of his muscles.

"Thank you," I whisper. His hand moves over my breast, thumb rolling my nipple in just the right way to make me gasp. I turn my face to his, a moan slipping free when his mouth finds my lips, the kiss deep and urgent.

"God, Kat," he growls. "You and your secrets...I ought to punish you for that."

My pussy clenches at his words. "Maybe you should," I tease back. But my heart hammers, and I know it's time. No more delaying.

I twist my body enough so that I can press my palms to his chest as I look him in the eye. The hunger in his gaze burns, but he frowns slightly at my sudden retreat.

"What is it?"

Here we go.

My stomach twists. "Pavel, there is one more secret I've been keeping from you." I swallow hard before saying, "I'm pregnant."

For a heartbeat, he just stares at me. Then he lets out a sharp breath, eyes blown wide.

"Pregnant?" he repeats, low and disbelieving. Shock and confusion flash across his face. I brace for anger next. But it doesn't come. Instead, joy takes over his features like sunlight.

"You're pregnant?" he says, grinning. "You really are full of surprises, aren't you?"

Tears blur my vision as I rub his chest. "I was scared to tell you. You have so much going on right now—"

He silences me with a heated kiss, his lips molding to mine. "Stop," he whispers, breaking away just enough to speak. "We'll figure it out. We already have a daughter, and now another baby is on the way. I've never been this goddamn happy."

I laugh, tears of joy streaming down my face while the bubbles float around us. He curves a hand over my belly, still grinning in awe. I kiss him again, this time more gently, letting the revelation settle.

"Thank you for telling me," he whispers against my mouth. "Now, no more secrets, okay?"

My lips turn upward into a smile. "No more."

A shiver of anticipation rolls down my spine when he slides one hand up my body, and his palm curves around my breast, fingertips grazing my nipple. I gasp at the electric jolt that shoots through me.

He trails his fingers down, sliding them between my thighs under the water, finding me slick and ready. He cups my pussy, teasing my clit with his thumb.

A ragged moan escapes my throat. I push against his palm, urging more contact. He shifts my body so that I'm in front of him again, on his lap. He presses his cock against my opening, teasing me.

"You want this?" he murmurs near my ear, biting my earlobe just enough to send a jolt of pleasure through me.

"Fuck, yes," I breathe. "Please."

He holds me up, sliding his tip against my entrance, and I whimper. My arms tremble, braced against the tub's edge. Slowly, he sinks inside, inch by inch, until he's fully buried. We both groan, the warmth of the water only adding to the pleasure.

"God, Kat," he says, pulling me tighter against his chest. "Every damn time, you feel so damn good."

My nails scrape the porcelain. The steam makes everything slick and hazy, the bathroom lights shimmering off the bubbles floating around us. He grips my hips, beginning a slow rhythm, each thrust more intense as he deliciously stretches me.

The drag of him inside me is almost too much, and my mind blanks. I ride the wave hard, pleasure coiling low in my belly until it snaps. My entire body tenses as I come, a choked cry ripping from my throat. Pavel's own orgasm follows, and he growls against my ear as he drains himself deep within.

For a moment, the only sounds are our ragged breathing and the slow deflation of the bubbles. My limbs go limp, the only movement the aftershocks rippling through me. His strong arms slide around my waist, pulling me back so my spine rests against his chest. My heart is still racing, my skin oversensitive.

He dips his head to kiss my shoulder, moving his lips up the line of my neck. "You okay?"

"More than okay," I reply. But something about the finality in his tone tells me he thinks we're done. A flicker of mischief sparks in my chest—I'm not done yet, not by a long shot.

I twist in his arms, the water swirling around us, foam clinging to our skin. His gaze slides over my body, a glint of surprise crossing his features when I plant my hands on his chest, pushing him back against the opposite side of the tub.

"Oh?" he says, brow lifting. "Feeling greedy?"

"Maybe," I mutter, letting a smile curve my lips. The need inside me hasn't been fully quenched. It's shifted into a different edge, a craving for more closeness, more sensation.

He braces his arms along the edge of the tub, watching me with dark intensity. "I warned you not to tempt me," he growls, a playful warning in his tone.

"Punish me, then," I tease, sliding closer. I can feel the water cooling, but I don't care. All I sense is the heat of him, the way his cock twitches as I settle my hips over his.

He answers by cupping the back of my neck and pulling me in for a searing kiss. "Stay like this," he whispers against my mouth. "I want to see you on top of me."

I lower myself onto him, his cock sliding inside me slowly. I moan at the stretch, at the wet glide, at the slight ache that melts into pleasure. He grips my waist, guiding me to sink lower, until he's fully sheathed. My nails bite into the porcelain as I adjust to the sensation.

"Fuck," he mutters, kneading my ass. "You take me so well."

He digs his fingers into my hips, urging me to move faster. "That's it," he says through gritted teeth.

I lean forward, arms locked, letting him control the angle and rhythm as I rock against him. The friction jolts through me, still so sensitive from the first orgasm. Each thrust forces a gasp from my lips, every nerve taut. He plunges even deeper.

Pleasure builds sharply, and I realize that I'm about to come again. I arch my back, tilting my head backward with a ragged moan. He grips my shoulder, pulling me close enough so his teeth can graze my neck in a gentle bite, the possessive gesture making me shudder.

"Kat," he hisses. "Come for me."

I let out a broken cry, my second orgasm slamming through me in hot waves. My inner walls clamp around him, and I hear him groan my name. His cock throbs, hips thrusting in desperate jolts until he goes rigid beneath me, releasing a guttural sound of raw satisfaction. I feel him spilling into me, hot and pulsing, triggering a final echo of pleasure in my own overstimulated body.

For a long moment, we stay like that, breathing as if we've just run a marathon, water rippling around us. Eventually, I ease forward, letting him slip free. My limbs tremble, exhaustion swirling in my veins. The tub is well past lukewarm now, but his body heat is enough.

I shift again, and he gently pulls me back against his chest, wrapping his arms around me so we can both rest. Our hearts begin to calm their rhythm, the scent of lingering lavender drifting around us. I close my eyes as the last tremors fade.

He kisses my shoulder, then nudges me to tilt my head so he can press his lips to mine. It's soft and loving—an odd contrast to the raw intensity we just shared. My chest tightens with affection and relief. We've conquered yet another hurdle in our relationship, forging a deeper bond than before.

We lay there, catching our breath, reveling in the quiet. I think of the joy on his face when I told him I was pregnant. My heart stutters with gratitude that he's not angry, not resentful, just simply happy. Finally, he says, "We should get out before we freeze."

I grin lazily. "We definitely destroyed the bathroom. We're going to need a lot of extra towels."

He chuckles. "Worth it."

Slowly, we untangle ourselves, standing on shaky legs. He helps me climb out first, then grabs a towel. My cheeks flush as he wraps it around me, his knuckles brushing the side of my breast tenderly.

He steps out, a towel slung around his hips. We look around the bathroom and exchange a wry smile as if to say, *what now?*

"We've got this," he says simply, pulling me close for another quick kiss. "And I don't mean just the bathroom. All of it. The Bratva. Piotr. Everything. Especially this baby."

My throat constricts, tears threatening. I swallow them down, nodding. "Together."

He nods back. "But next time you keep something from me, Kat, I'll spank you twice as hard."

"Promise?" I respond playfully.

He laughs. "You're trouble."

"Maybe," I admit, letting him guide me toward the bedroom, leaving behind a trail of water and scattered bubbles on the floor. "But you wouldn't have me any other way."

His hand settles on the small of my back, warm and solid. "Damn right."

His eyes flick over my face before pressing a gentle kiss to my forehead. "This Bratva mess, Piotr, the Novikovs...I promise I'll keep our family safe."

Our family. Two words I don't think I'll ever get tired of hearing. But there's still one more lie left, one more secret. And it just might be the one that tears us apart for good.

But one I have to reveal to him all the same.

CHAPTER 30

PAVEL

I lie in bed, staring at the dark ceiling.

Kat's breathing is slow and even beside me, but my mind refuses to shut down. Every time I close my eyes, I'm bombarded by thoughts of Piotr, the Novikovs, and everything that threatens the sanctity of our home. Even though Kat and Ana are safe under this roof, I can't shake the feeling that I need to act soon, before everything unravels and becomes too dangerous.

I slip out from under the covers as quietly as I can. Kat murmurs something unintelligible, her brow creasing for an instant before settling again. I brush my fingertips lightly over her hair, fighting the urge to shake her awake just to have her reassure me that everything will be fine.

But she's been through enough, and she needs sleep to keep herself and the baby healthy. I pull on a T-shirt and lounge pants, then pad down the hallway in bare feet. The place is silent, every shadow lengthened in the moonlight. It shouldn't be so still; one of the guards is usually posted near the end of the hall. I clench my jaw at the sight of the empty corridor.

I'll deal with that later. Right now, I just need some space to think.

My office is dim, the curtains drawn. I switch on the desk lamp and cross to the bar cart. I pour a splash of whiskey into a tumbler, just enough to take the edge off. I rest against the desk, glass in hand, letting my mind go to things I don't want to think about but need to.

Piotr. Novikov. Both are threats I can't afford to ignore, especially not now, when I have more to lose than ever. Kat is my wife, and now there's Ana, our daughter, plus the baby on the way. The mere thought of someone trying to harm them makes me want to put my fist through a wall—or through Piotr's skull.

I sip the whiskey, letting the sharp burn ground me. My best move might be to bypass Piotr altogether and go straight to Viktor Novikov and his right-hand man. If I can force a meeting, I'll make a show of strength, so they realize going against me is a losing proposition.

Vlad asked for a couple of days to gather intel, to see if he could uncover more proof that Piotr orchestrated these attacks. I told him I'd wait, but every hour that passes feels like a chance for Piotr to dig deeper trenches around us.

Vlad had Ana and Camille's things sent over, as promised. No doubt Piotr's going to notice that two rooms in their house are empty, and when he does, he'll know that something is afoot.

Conflict is coming, but for now, my girls are safe.

I take another sip, the liquid burning my throat. Piotr's always been ambitious, but now he's stepped over a line, using Ana as leverage, trying to sow discord. He'll bring war to our families, if we let this drag on for much longer. I'd rather take the fight to him than wait like a sitting duck for it to come to me. Kat asked me to be patient, and I agreed for her sake—for now.

"Hey." Kat's voice cuts through the storm of my thoughts.

She's wearing one of my button-downs, the hem hitting mid-thigh, barely covering her long, toned legs. It falls off one shoulder, exposing her smooth skin, the curve of her collarbone. Her hair is wild from sleep, she's barefoot, and she looks tired, her eyelids still heavy. Even exhausted, she's the most beautiful thing I've ever seen.

She leans against the doorframe, watching me. "Couldn't sleep?"

I down the last of my whiskey, letting the heat settle in my chest. "Too much to think about." My gaze rakes down her body, slow and deliberate. "You should be in bed."

She tilts her head, the faintest smirk playing on her lips. "So should you."

I set the glass down. "It's been a busy night."

"I know." She lingers near the door, as if uncertain whether she's allowed to approach.

I stand up from the desk, but she lifts a hand, stopping me. "Wait," she says softly.

Something in her expression makes my stomach clench. "What is it?"

I can see she's trembling. "I have one more confession, and I need to tell you before this goes any further."

"Go on."

She inhales a shaky breath then holds out her hand. In it is a small glass vial. It catches the lamplight, the liquid inside nearly colorless. Tears fill her eyes.

"What is that?" I ask. But I already know.

"Poison."

The word hangs in the air.

"Piotr gave me this," she says. "He wanted me to kill you on our wedding night."

A flash of fury lances through me. I stare at the vial before looking up at her tear-streaked cheeks. I clench my fists as I recall everything that happened that night, the fear in her eyes, the way she seemed distant afterward.

"He told you to kill me," I echo, the words coming out in a bitter snarl. "And you agreed?"

Tears slide down her cheeks. "I was stupid, angry, misguided. It was ingrained in me that your family was responsible for the death of my parents. Piotr convinced me it was the only way to get revenge. But when it came down to it, I couldn't do it. I've kept the vial hidden ever since."

I take a deep breath, releasing it slowly, forcing myself to keep my voice level. "Why didn't you throw it away? Destroy it?"

She shrugs helplessly, tears still falling. "I couldn't face it, I guess. I needed to remember how close I came to making the worst decision of my life. I never intended to use it."

Part of me wants to lash out at her, at the fact that she kept yet another secret from me. But there's another part, one that recognizes the fear she's been carrying, one that knows she's telling me because she trusts me now.

"You should have told me sooner."

She nods, swallowing. "I know. I'm sorry. I was afraid you'd never forgive me."

I pluck the vial from her fingers, my gaze fixed on the lethal contents. I reach for her shoulder with my free hand, drawing her closer. I glare down at the tiny vial in my hand, my jaw tight. "You're forgiven," I say coldly. I toss the damn thing into the trash. "It's done."

Kat releases a shaky breath, tears spilling over onto my shirt. "You're not angry?"

"I am," I snap, "but not with you, not anymore. He used you, your grief, your loyalty. That's on Piotr."

A half-broken laugh escapes her, one I can only imagine is relief. "Thank you." She tilts her head back and wipes her cheeks, eyes glistening. "I love you."

Something hot sparks in my chest. I take her face in my hands, leaning in for a kiss that starts gentle then grows desperate. "I love you, too, and I swear, I'll fix all of this. He won't touch you ever again."

She clings to me, kissing me back fiercely through her tears. My body hums with the urge to take her back to our room, show her just how much I love her, but then we hear a crash downstairs.

We both freeze. Kat instinctively steps toward the office door, but I quickly grab her arm. I have security posted. Nobody should be getting close enough to break into my penthouse at this hour—or ever.

"Stay here," I hiss, yanking out my phone. The camera feed shows my guard lying on the floor near the door, his legs sticking out. My pulse spikes. I can't tell whether he's dead or just unconscious. A wave of cold rage runs through me.

"Pavel?" Kat whispers. "What's happening?"

"Get Ana and Camille," I command, my tone leaving no room for argument. "Go to the panic room, lock it, and don't come out until I say."

She pales but doesn't argue. "What about you?"

I'm already texting my men.

Breach. Now.

"Help is on the way."

Before I can say anything else, a small explosion from downstairs echoes up the hall.

Kat yelps, fear in her eyes. I toss my phone aside, stepping in front of her as a swarm of at least a dozen armed men barrels into my office, their weapons aimed right at us. My mind spins.

Where the hell is my security detail?

"Get on the floor!" one of them barks, the muzzle of his gun pointed at my chest.

Fury boils within, but Kat's right behind me, pressed against my back. If I try something, they'll shoot her. I raise my hands slowly.

One intruder steps forward, jabbing his rifle at us. "Down! Now!"

I ease myself to my knees, pulling Kat down with me. I clench my jaw so hard it hurts. Masked strangers are taking over my home. Kat's breath is shaky. I'm dying to lash out, but I can't risk them turning their guns on her.

How the hell did this happen?

The men shout at each other as they form a perimeter. Another stares me down, his weapon inches from my face. I managed to hit send on that text, but it might be too late.

One of them yells, "Hands behind your head! Don't fucking move!"

They force me onto my stomach, one of them smashing my phone beneath their boot. I snarl inwardly. My last link to help—gone. Pain rips through me when a rifle butt cracks against my shoulder. Kat cries out in fear, but they tell her to shut up. My mind roars with the urge to kill them all, but I stay still, swallowing the rage.

I'm yanked upright, my arms wrenched behind my back. Fire spreads through my muscles. I steal a quick look at Kat —she's in the same state, trembling and restrained. The men bark orders to each other, scanning the halls for any other targets. If any of my guards are still alive, they're nowhere to be found.

One of the men steps in front of me. "Where's the rest of your family?"

I refuse to answer. He jerks my arms higher, pain burning down my spine. Kat stifles a sob beside me. I meet her eyes, trying to project calm, but inside, I'm fuming. If they so much as touch her...

Suddenly, they push both of us back down on our knees. The muzzle of a gun presses to my temple.

Ana had better be with Camille, I think, a red haze edging my vision. My unborn child, my wife, my daughter: Everything that matters to me is in jeopardy.

"Tell me where everyone else is," another man snarls at me.

I keep my mouth shut. He tries again, but I only glare. I grunt as the butt of a rifle slams into my ribs. My head spins with agony, but still I don't answer. Kat whimpers, tears streaming down her face. She's terrified. I can't afford to look weak; men like this thrive on fear.

The leader steps forward, gun at my face. "Tell us now, or you're both dead."

"Fuck you."

He presses the barrel against my cheek. Kat's cries, ripping my heart in half. But I won't tell them anything.

In the back of my mind, one single thought screams: *My men better show up soon, or we're dead.*

But if these bastards find Ana, if they dare harm what's mine, I swear I'll rip them apart with my bare hands. For now, though, I bide my time on the floor, breathing through the pain, letting them think they have the upper hand.

Because a cornered man with everything to lose is the most dangerous man alive.

CHAPTER 31

KAT

My heart pounds so fiercely in my ears that I can barely hear anything else.

All around me, harsh voices echo off the walls as armed men stomp across the floors of Pavel's home—our home. I fight to steady my breaths, forcing myself not to hyperventilate. I can't crumble. I need to protect Ana, Camille, and the baby I'm carrying. But I don't dare let my mind fixate on them too long. Doing so would unravel my nerves completely, rendering me helpless.

I am not helpless.

Instead, I focus on staying calm, on watching every movement these intruders make, searching for a weakness where I can fight back or flee. Pavel said that help is on the way. I believe him. I have to. Perhaps he managed to send a text before the intruders blew the door open, or maybe his men have realized something is off by now. Either way, I cling to the hope that we're not alone.

My gaze drifts to the hallway, my heart twisting in fear.

Ana.

My daughter is with Camille, and I pray they haven't been found. If these men locate them, I don't know what will happen. I swallow down a wave of terror as I glimpse a flicker of movement by the door. A man steps inside.

Piotr.

A chill blasts through me, so cold that the hair on my arms stands up. I've seen my brother do terrible things before, but never an open assault on his own family. This is raw, blatant, and intentional violence.

All rational thought flees, replaced by anger, incandescent and unstoppable. It roars inside me. The next thing I know, I'm lunging to my feet, ignoring every shred of caution, in an attempt to launch myself at my traitorous brother. A furious scream rips from my throat before I can stop it.

"Piotr!"

I might as well be a leaf trying to knock down a wall. Two men intercept me easily. They tighten their grip on my arms. A sharp pain radiates through my shoulders, halting my momentum. I thrash, refusing to give in, but they're too strong. My feet barely skid across the polished floor.

Out of the corner of my eye, I see Pavel move. It's a blink of motion, a flash of raw fury. In an instant, he's upon them, but there are too many. Another one of the masked men leaps forward, ramming a fist into Pavel's ribs. Someone else grabs him around the neck. It takes three men, bigger than him and straining with the effort, to subdue him. Yet Pavel still manages to crack one in the jaw before they slam him to the floor.

"Don't you touch her!" he roars, voice thick with rage. Blood drips from his split lip. My chest tightens, and I don't know whether to be furious or terrified or both.

Piotr laughs, a cold, hollow sound that turns my blood to ice. He steps closer, his demeanor calm as if this is just a usual encounter, and I can't help but feel a flicker of revulsion. The men around us stiffen at his presence, making space for him.

"Leave us alone!" I spit at him.

"Little sister," Piotr says, his voice full of mocking amusement. "You're in no position to make demands."

He reaches out, patting my cheek. Not gently either, it's more like a slap, and it stings. Pavel fights to sit upright, but all he gets are more fists and more shouts. My heart aches.

Piotr draws back, meeting Pavel's furious glare with a smirk. "Soon enough, everything will be under my control, but for now," he waves a hand like he's bored, looking around the room, "I want a word with my dear brother-in-law." He smirks at me. "And with you, Kat."

I wrestle against the men's grips, but they hold me fast. They're well-trained, or at least well-motivated, because none of them give an inch.

My mind whirls with fear and anger, my only thought is of my daughter; she has to be safe. I pray Camille heard the commotion and found a place to hide. If these men get their hands on my daughter...

My brother crosses the room to Pavel's desk and makes himself comfortable in the big leather chair. He leans back like he owns the place. His casual posture enrages me.

He gestures to the two chairs on the other side of the desk. "Sit."

The men holding me shove me forward, releasing my arms. My shoulders scream in pain, and for a moment, I can't move them properly. They raise Pavel to a standing position. I can see the purple smudge forming around his right eye, the blood on his lip. Yet he stands tall, adjusting his shirt like it's a normal day.

His composure is unnerving—maybe that's the point. He meets Piotr's smug grin with cold detachment, and a spike of pride flickers in my chest. My brave husband, calm in the face of chaos, refusing to give Piotr the satisfaction of seeing any fear.

We take the seats, me on the left, Pavel on the right. Piotr sighs dramatically. "You have no idea how tired I am of waiting for you both to learn your place."

"Spare me the monolog," Pavel bites back, voice as icy as his glare. "Tell me what you want, or is this just a petty display of power you orchestrated to impress your new friends?"

Piotr chuckles. "You'll see soon enough. My 'new friends' are already reaping benefits." He leans forward on the desk, hands folded. "But let's not get ahead of ourselves. We need to talk."

I glance at Pavel, who's glaring at Piotr with lethal intent. Piotr wants a conversation, presumably to gloat or threaten. What's his endgame? And even if we manage to endure his show, what of the men who came with him? Are they all part of the Novikov Bratva or just hired guns?

There's a scuffle of footsteps and the sound of grunting comes from the hallway. My head snaps toward the office door. Someone is being hauled in forcibly. Pavel tenses, half-standing. "Who—"

The men by the office door step aside and my stomach lurches at the sight: Vlad. Two men practically drag him over the threshold. He's hunched over, his face a mess of bruises, one eye swollen shut, lip split. When they reach the middle of the room, they let him go, and he collapses on the floor in a heap.

I lurch to my feet with a cry, ignoring the guns that jerk in my direction. "Vlad!"

He tries to push himself up on trembling arms, but his strength fails. I rush forward, tears burning my vision. The men aim rifles at me, but I don't care. I cradle Vlad's face, seeing the extent of the damage up close. "Oh my God," I whisper, voice trembling. "Vlad..."

He manages a broken, breathless chuckle. "It's not as bad as it looks." Blood coats his teeth, making the words almost unintelligible. My vision blurs with rage.

I spin around, glaring at Piotr as I yell, "Piotr, what have you done?"

CHAPTER 32

PAVEL

Kat's voice is weak, her heart clearly broken at the sight of Vlad's condition.

He's sprawled on the floor, barely conscious. Blood stains his cheek, and his battered face has swelled so badly that one of his eyes is practically sealed shut. My stomach knots at the sight of him.

He tries to mumble something else, but his words come out in a broken wheeze.

Kat kneels beside him, tears streaming down her cheeks, one hand supporting his head in her lap. I want to rush over and help, see how badly he's hurt, but the close presence of two armed men pins me in place. Their rifles hover too close for comfort, both pointed in my general direction, ready to fire if I so much as twitch.

Kat's voice trembles. "He's your brother," she chokes out, brushing her free hand against Vlad's temple. "Your own blood. How could you do this?"

Her eyes look over the other injuries littering his body. He's been beaten; every ragged breath he takes is clearly painful. I'm guessing his ribs are broken.

Piotr sits comfortably at my desk, watching her meltdown with a dismissiveness that churns my stomach. His posture is rigid, arms folded over his chest, as if that alone proves he's in charge.

Kat's tears dampen her jawline. "Look at him!" she demands, pointing at Vlad's swollen face. "You think this is okay? You think—"

"Shut the fuck up," Piotr snaps, cutting her off. "He's not dead, is he? You're lucky I let him live this long." He waves one hand like Vlad's life is an afterthought.

Anger surges through me and I clench my fists at my sides, forcing myself not to lunge forward and tear Piotr's throat out. If I do, these gunmen will shoot.

Kat's grief morphs into fury. "You're a monster!" she spits, tears still shining on her cheeks. "I thought you were cruel before, but this, your own brother—"

"I said shut up!" Piotr glances her way, his face darkening. "I've had enough of your mouth, Kat. One more word, and I'll allow one of my men to handle you."

"Don't threaten my wife," I hiss, menace in my tone. One of the armed men takes a half-step toward me. He lifts his rifle, but I don't give him the satisfaction of even flinching.

Piotr stares back at me, lips curling in a malevolent grin. "If you haven't noticed, you're in no position to give orders, Fetisov. One wrong move and I put a bullet in her, then you."

Kat's gaze darts to me and I see the question in her eyes. *Are we truly helpless here?*

"You disappoint me, Piotr."

He scoffs. "As if I care. You're not my father."

I take a breath. "No," I say, letting my voice drop. "He's dead, because you killed him."

A stifled sob slips from Kat. Vlad, half-unconscious, tries to lift his head. I can see confusion and horror in his one open eye. Out in the hallway, I hear footsteps as men shuffle around, likely ensuring no reinforcements can get in. I can only hope that Nikolai got my text.

Piotr's composure cracks for a split second. "You think I didn't have my reasons?" he snarls. "I did what I had to do. The old man was too stuck in alliances and mergers, business shit. He would've let the city slip away. So yeah, I sent that truck to slam into their car. It was a swift end for old-fashioned fools."

Kat's strangled sobs tear at my heart. Vlad chokes out a half groan, half murmur of disbelief. The heartbreak in their faces is so raw, I can almost feel it in my own bones.

"You murdered our parents!" Kat shouts. "Do you even care?"

"Our mother was simply in the wrong place at the wrong time," Piotr answers dismissively. "Collateral damage. I did what had to be done."

Vlad coughs, and Kat strokes his hair again, trying to calm him. He's in terrible shape; it's a miracle he's even conscious.

My head pounds, searching for a way out of this. Piotr's men are everywhere. We're unarmed, and we've just heard his explicit confession to double homicide. He won't let us live if we keep pressing him.

Piotr shifts in the chair, crossing his arms again. Men with rifles remain near the door, forming a barrier. He glances between Kat and me. "So now you know. And now I have to decide if it's worth it to let you live."

Kat swallows, tears still flowing, but fury has taken over her expression. She's lost so much already. Vlad clings to her side, wounded, in and out of consciousness. My mind races with the possibility that if we can hold Piotr's attention a while longer, maybe my men can break through. But that's a big maybe.

"You plan on killing all of us," I say. It's not a question. I can see it in his eyes that he's leaning that way.

He doesn't confirm or deny, he only sneers. That answers me well enough. If he was confident in sparing us, he'd play the benevolent victor. Instead, he just sits there, bristling with tension. He wants total power. No survivors.

I steel my voice, forcing a level tone. "If you do that, you'll face the entire Fetisov Bratva seeking revenge. The Andreev men loyal to Vlad will turn on you if they discover the truth about your father. And there's a good chance the Novikovs will swoop in to tear up a weakened city. You'll lose everything."

He scowls, brushing his fingertips along the desk. "I can handle them," he says, but I catch the flicker of doubt in his eyes. He knows how risky a multi-front war would be.

Kat's cheeks are wet, but she can't tear her gaze from Piotr. "Handle them? You think murdering everyone solves everything?"

"Watch your mouth," he snaps, but there's no real energy behind it this time. "If you hadn't stuck your nose in—"

I cut him off. "That's not the point. The city will burn if you push this further. Kat and Vlad aren't just random people, they're Andreev royalty, just like you. They have loyalists, too."

Piotr's men shift around uneasily. The hush weighs heavily. I keep my posture relaxed, though my gut is twisting. If I push too hard, he might snap. But I have to propose something.

"Send your men out," I say. "Let's talk privately. No need for them to overhear. You want real power? You want a city that won't turn into a war zone? We can negotiate or are you so far gone that you'd rather swim in blood?"

His gaze flicks to Vlad's battered form, to the tears staining Kat's cheeks. He exhales sharply, the tension crackling. For a moment, I think he's going to reject me outright. But then he jerks his chin at his men. "Out. Wait in the hall."

The leader hesitates, gun lowering slightly. "Boss—"

"Go," Piotr growls, glaring until they shuffle out, rifles at the ready as they step into the corridor. The door remains ajar, but the immediate threat is gone. Relief seeps into my lungs.

Kat still cradles Vlad, who's breathing in shallow, pained bursts. Piotr glances up at me, guarded. "Fine. Talk. What's your brilliant plan, Fetisov? Come on—your life depends on it."

CHAPTER 33

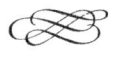

KAT

"Alright, Piotr," Pavel says. "Let's talk."

Vlad's bloodshot gaze flicks to me as I adjust my hand beneath his head. He's trembling, bruised everywhere, and barely able to stay alert, but still insists it's not as bad as it looks.

"Vlad," I whisper, "do you think you can stand?"

He breathes a ragged breath. "I'll manage." His mouth curls, like he's forcing a grin through the swelling. "Just...give me a hand."

I slide my shoulder under his arm and haul him up, worried I won't be able to hold his weight. He groans softly, and I fight to keep him from collapsing back onto the floor. The battered look in his eye crushes me, but there's a flash of pride there—he refuses to be seen as helpless.

Piotr sits at Pavel's desk, arms folded, posture rigid. His men hover just outside the door, rifles ready. My pulse pounds in my ears. Across the room, Pavel watches as I struggle to help Vlad, and I know there's fiery anger simmering under his calm demeanor.

"Vlad," Pavel cautions, "take it slow."

Vlad nods stiffly, leaning into me. Then, with a faint cough, he lifts his head toward Piotr. "We need to talk as a family, not as enemies," he manages, though his voice is weak.

Piotr's mouth curls in contempt. "Family? That's funny." His eyes drift over Vlad, then me, then Pavel. "I won't have any family left after tonight."

Vlad's weight shifts against me. I can feel the tremor in his muscles. He's struggling to stay upright, but his glare is unwavering. I grit my teeth, rage boiling within. Pavel steps forward, shoulders squared.

"Piotr," Pavel says, "we can still work this out without shedding more blood. You know—"

Piotr glares at Pavel. "Work it out? I'm done with your fake negotiations. I made a deal with Viktor Novikov. We take you out, then the city is ours."

My stomach twists. "You'd betray everything our father built?" I choke out, ignoring the tears that threaten to spill. "You're a piece of shit, Piotr. Dad must be rolling in his grave."

He barks a harsh laugh. "Rolling in ashes, you mean," he corrects, eyes blazing. "He's gone. Get over it. And once I kill Pavel, no one will be able to stand against Viktor and me. Not you, not Vlad, not any of the old guard."

I'm so angry, I feel like my nerves are on fire. Next to me, Vlad continues to tremble, his nails biting into my shoulder.

"You—" he tries, but words fail him. His voice cracks. "Brother, I loved you once, you bastard."

Piotr's jaw twitches but he doesn't acknowledge Vlad's pain outright. Instead, he turns to Pavel. "Do you think there's some sort of compromise coming?"

Pavel keeps his composure, though I sense his fury in the way his fists clench at his sides. "We don't have to do this. More killing, more war, will only—"

"There's no compromise," Piotr snarls. He jerks his head at one of his men standing in the hallway, anxiously awaiting direction. The thug steps forward, pressing a handgun into Piotr's palm.

My heart drops. Pavel tenses, bracing himself.

Piotr stands and lifts the gun, leveling it at Pavel's head. I can't breathe. Time seems to freeze—until my body moves on instinct.

"No!" I shout, shoving Vlad's arm off me and hurling myself in front of Pavel. My arms go up as fear and adrenaline coil in my gut. "You'll have to kill me first."

"Kat, move!" Pavel growls behind me, grabbing at my waist. He tries to yank me out of the line of fire, but I grip the edge of the desk in an attempt to anchor myself.

Piotr's gun remains fixed on Pavel's head.

"You're both idiots," he says as he looks at me with an ugly sneer. "Fine. I'll start with you since you won't step aside.

Doesn't matter anyway. What a disappointment you turned out to be, little sister."

I swallow hard, forcing my voice to remain steady. "Think about Ana. She's your niece. She looks up to you; she adores you. Do you want her to grow up knowing you killed her parents?" The words come out almost frantically, my throat nearly closing up as I say them.

His lip curls into a wicked sneer. "Ana will be safe. I'll see to that. She doesn't need an idiotic mother who stands in front of bullets. Now step away, or I'll shoot through you."

Pavel's arms circle my waist, again trying to pull me back.

"Damn it, Kat," he grits out. "Don't—"

I twist free. "No." My heart hammers. "Piotr, if you do this, you'll destroy her."

He barks a humorless laugh. "Oh, I'm sure she'll manage. She won't even remember you in a few years. This is your last warning."

Time seems to slow down.

Vlad lets out a hoarse cry. I don't see him clearly, but I sense his movement. Maybe he's trying to lunge at Piotr or maybe he's collapsing from the pain. Pavel tugs me sideways, cursing, desperation in his eyes as he locks them on mine. But my feet refuse to budge from Piotr's line of fire.

Piotr's eyes flash with a cruel darkness as he adjusts his grip on the gun, taking aim again, this time directly at me. My stomach clenches in terror.

Behind me, Vlad coughs and tries to shout. At the same instant, Pavel lunges, trying to push me out of the way.

Piotr's expression looks savage, his finger tightening on the trigger.

He fires.

The gunshot explodes like thunder.

CHAPTER 34

PAVEL

Everything happens so fast.

I hear the crack of a gunshot as Vlad lunges forward with what little strength he has left, his body jerking to the side, blood blooming on his shoulder. He collapses, letting out a strangled cry that cuts straight into my gut.

"Vlad!" Kat's scream echoes through the noise. She's at his side in an instant, pressing her hands to the wound. My stomach twists at the sight of his blood staining her fingers.

"What the hell have you done, you prick?" I growl at Piotr.

He's standing with the gun still raised, a maniacal expression on his face, like something inside him has finally snapped.

"It's almost finished," he says as he points the gun at me again.

A shot rings out from somewhere in the distance, then another, and another. I hear shouting.

"What the hell?" Piotr says in confusion.

More gunfire sounds from downstairs, and I hear men shouting orders at one another in Russian. One of Piotr's men pokes his head into the room.

"Boss, we're under attack!"

I grin. Nikolai. He made it. And from the sound of it, he brought a whole goddamn army with him.

"Fuck!" Piotr shouts.

Piotr's men pour into the room, taking cover, and firing back while my men gain ground.

I dash across the room, dragging Vlad behind my desk and shouting at Kat to join us. She's trembling, terror written all over her expression. Piotr and his men continue to exchange gunfire with Nikolai and his team. He throws a coffee table onto its side, taking cover behind it as he continues to fire. Several of his men fall down around him.

I open a compartment on the underside of my desk, taking out a pistol. Then, I turn my attention to Vlad. He's bleeding profusely and looking paler by the second.

"Keep pressure on the wound," I bark at Kat over the deafening blasts.

My heart hammers as I flatten a hand on top of hers, forcing more pressure onto Vlad's shoulder to stem the bleeding.

Vlad groans and his eyes roll back. I grit my teeth. "Don't pass out," I order, though I'm not sure he can even hear me.

Bullets whine overhead, splinters from a demolished shelf pepper my back.

"Stay down!" I shout to Kat, shifting my body to shield them both.

She hunches down, practically lying across Vlad, tears dripping onto his face. Another hail of gunfire cracks through the air, lighting up the room in staccato bursts. I can barely think, the pounding of my pulse in my ears is almost as deafening as the gunfire.

"What's happening?" Kat asks.

I hunch lower as another barrage of bullets fly. A thick haze of gunfire smoke fills the room. "Nikolai," I cough out. "He's here with our men."

A thunderous burst of shotgun fire resonates from the hallway. I peer around the corner of the desk and spot movement—more black-clad figures moving into the room. I can't tell whether they are mine or Piotr's. Another volley of shots rips through the doorway; bullets pepper the walls.

My gaze darts to the side and I spot Piotr, his pistol raised. His face is twisted in a mix of rage and desperation. He trains the gun on Kat, who's lying over Vlad, pressing her body weight onto his wound, her arms slick with Vlad's blood.

Dread freezes my blood. "No," I growl, pivoting in place, ignoring the bullets whizzing overhead. I steady my own gun with both hands. I won't let him kill her. He's already destroyed so much. He orchestrated this entire nightmare.

I align my shot with his forehead, and I pull the trigger.

The single shot roars in my ears. Piotr's head snaps back, eyes going wide. He remains upright for a fraction of a second, as though refusing to accept that he's just been shot between the eyes.

He finally collapses, his body crumpling across broken furniture. I pull in a shaky breath, my mind reeling. Piotr is gone. My old friend. Kat's brother.

The gunfire continues but it's now less concentrated. A few final bursts come from the far side of the hall, and I realize those must be the last of Piotr's men. Over the next minute or so, everything quiets. I crouch down, helping Kat with the pressure on Vlad's wound. He's barely conscious, blood still pulsing beneath our hands. Kat's frantic but determined, refusing to let him slip away.

Suddenly, a hush falls over the room. My ears are still ringing from the onslaught, every nerve twitching in readiness for more shots, but the corridor remains eerily quiet. I lift my head, scanning the room. Broken furniture, bullet holes, bodies. My office has been completely destroyed.

The stench of gunpowder, blood, and death saturates the air. Men in black vests edge in, rifles lowered, carefully checking for survivors. I recognize them as my own, Nikolai's team.

"All clear," one calls out, stepping over a corpse near the doorway. "Boss, you in here?"

I exhale, heart pounding. "Here!" I yell back. "Get a medic—Vlad's hit!"

Nikolai emerges from the smoky hall, eyes wide with alarm. He sees Kat and I pinned down over Vlad, my body braced protectively in front of them.

"Christ," he mutters, gesturing two men forward. "Get him to a doctor."

Kat refuses to budge until they physically ease her aside. She cries out, letting go of Vlad's shoulder with trembling hands. Blood coats her palms, her shirt, her tear-streaked cheeks. I swallow a wave of nausea at the sight but manage to help her up.

Vlad moans, eyelids fluttering when the men shift him onto a makeshift plank. His wounded arm dangles limply, and my gut seizes with fear that we might be too late. He's still breathing, but his condition is grave.

"Get him to a hospital now!" I snap at the men. "There's no time to waste."

They nod, carrying him gently but quickly through the wreckage. Kat hovers, wanting to follow, but I hold her in place.

"Wait," I tell her. "Let them handle it. You're in shock."

She wipes at her face, blinking rapidly as she glances around the room. That's when her gaze lands on Piotr's body, sprawled over a half-crushed coffee table. Her breath catches. She stares, torn between horror and heartbreak.

"Piotr," she whispers. "No..."

Guilt gnaws at me. I shot him to protect her, but seeing Kat's grief shreds me. She steps forward, slipping out of my grasp to go to his body. I quickly intercept, blocking her line of sight.

"Don't look," I say quietly.

She tries to push past me, tears glistening. "He was my brother," she chokes out. "I...just let me..."

I can't deny her. Reluctantly, I shift aside. Her eyes fix on Piotr's glassy stare, at the bullet hole in his forehead. She presses a hand to her mouth and sobs, a strangled sound ripping free. My heart aches for her. Piotr became a monster, but first, he was family.

Kat crouches down but she doesn't touch him. She only stares, her body shaking in silent sobs. A moment passes. I swallow hard as I place a hand on her shoulder. "I'm sorry," I say. The words feel woefully inadequate.

She nods, trembling. "I know he tried to kill us; I know he killed our parents..." Her voice breaks. "But he was still my brother."

I let out a slow breath, glancing around the ruined office. The place is unrecognizable. Bullet holes are everywhere, the furniture destroyed, bodies strewn across the floor. My men carefully step around the debris, checking to see if any of the attackers are still alive.

None of them is. Piotr's men paid the ultimate price for his ambition.

Kat's eyes flash with terror. "Ana, Camille. We need to find them! What if he sent men looking for them?" Her expression shatters anew at the potential reality.

"Oh God, Ana!" She looks around wildly. "Where is she? And Camille?

"We'll find them," I reassure her.

I'm sick with worry, but I don't let it show. I have to find my daughter.

Nothing else matters.

CHAPTER 35

PAVEL

"Come," I say softly, giving Kat's hand a squeeze. "Let's go find our daughter."

I gently guide her out of the office, not wanting her to linger over her brother's body. She glances back once, her lip trembling, then lets me lead her into the hallway.

The house is a wreck—overturned tables, pockmarked walls, shattered picture frames. Bullet casings glint under the recessed lighting as my men patrol the battered corridors, stepping over the twisted corpses of Piotr's men.

Kat's free hand fists against her mouth, her grief and anger taking over. Her eyes flick back and forth across the destruction, but she says nothing.

"Ana. What if Piotr's men..." She can't even finish the thought.

"Don't go there. We'll find her."

We push forward. The air is thick with the smell of gunpowder. A few of my men are going through the house, calling out to one another, checking corners and closets. Farther down the hall, I hear someone shout, "Clear!" Another voice calls, "No sign of them here!"

We keep searching.

Kat's steps slow as we approach Ana's bedroom. The door is riddled with bullet holes. She reaches for the knob, knuckles white. We brace ourselves and step inside. It's empty—no sign of a struggle, but no sign of our daughter either. My heart clenches as Kat's lips part in a silent question. *Where is she?*

"Camille probably hid her somewhere," I tell her. "Maybe they found the panic room."

Kat exhales shakily. "Right."

We hurry into Camille's room. The door stands ajar, the interior is trashed: clothes tossed, furniture broken. A dresser leans precariously against a wall. My stomach twists, imagining a fight here.

"Ana?" Kat calls. She skims the destruction with worried eyes. "Camille?"

We hear a faint shuffling noise coming from the corner. I raise my gun automatically before a soft voice says, "I...I am here."

Kat's eyes widen. "Camille."

We follow the voice to the other side of the bed. Kat rushes around and I'm right behind her. Camille emerges from beneath the bed, her cheek smeared with blood, hair disheveled. She clings to the bed frame for support, a mixture of relief and shock on her face.

"Camille," Kat gasps, kneeling to help her. "Are you hurt?"

She shakes her head, fresh bruises marring her face. "They hit me, demanded to know where Ana was, but I didn't tell them anything." Her voice breaks. "I said nothing."

"You did well." I help Camille to her feet. "Where is Ana?"

Camille glances toward a big, heavy dresser half shoved in front of a door. "She's locked in the bathroom. I blocked the door with that. I had no time to hide anywhere else before the gunfire started."

I stare at the massive oak piece. "You pushed that alone?"

She gives a shaky shrug. "I can't explain. Perhaps it was mama bear strength, yes?"

Kat takes a step toward the dresser, pressing her shoulder against it. I join her, ignoring the throbbing in my muscles from the earlier beating. Together, we manage to shift it aside. It screeches across the torn floorboards, revealing the bathroom door behind it.

Camille nods. "Ana locked herself inside. She wouldn't open up for me again."

Kat doesn't wait. She rushes to the doorknob, frantically rattling it.

"Ana?" she calls. "Baby, open up. It's Mama."

No response. I see a flicker of fear cross Kat's face. Without hesitation, I wedge my shoulder against the door. "Ana, honey, back away from the door," I warn softly.

Kat steps aside, and I ram it once, twice. The hinges groan, then splinter. One more shove, and the door swings open, revealing a dark bathroom. I flip on the switch, heart in my throat.

A small figure is curled up in the tub, arms wrapped around her knees. As the light flares, she lifts her head, eyes wet with tears. My chest clenches.

Ana.

The relief I feel at the sight of my daughter, unharmed after what just happened, is indescribable.

Kat lets out a sob. "Ana!" She runs forward, and our daughter leaps from the tub, launching into her mother's arms.

"Mama!" Ana cries. Kat holds her tight, tears pouring down her face. My vision blurs with unexpected emotion. After everything, we found her safe.

Camille sinks onto the bathtub's edge, pressing a hand to her mouth as if stifling a sob. "I told her it was hide-and-seek," she murmurs. "Told her not to open the door for anyone. They threatened me, but I wouldn't speak."

Kat, still clutching Ana, manages a broken thank you, leaning in to hug Camille with one arm.

My chest aches with gratitude.

I brush my palm across Ana's hair. "You okay, sweetheart?"

She sniffles, burying her face against Kat's neck. "I was so scared," she mumbles.

Kat soothes her with gentle strokes over her back. "It's over," she whispers. "No more shooting."

Camille stands, pushing her hair back. "What about Piotr?"

Kat's face crumples. I look at Camille and mouth the words *He's gone*.

Camille closes her eyes, nodding in resigned understanding as Kat carries Ana out of the bathroom.

"He tried to kill you, didn't he?"

I nod. "Yes, and he seriously hurt Vlad. He's on his way to the hospital now."

Ana shifts in Kat's arms as Camille and I enter the bedroom. She glances up at us with wide, worried eyes. She recognizes the names, picking up on the tension. "Where's Uncle Vlad?"

"Getting help," Kat says, giving her a brave smile that wavers at the edges. "He'll be okay."

We hope.

"We should leave. Go somewhere that isn't a damn war zone."

Kat nods, swallowing hard. She turns to Camille, noticing the bruises again. "You need medical attention, too."

Camille shakes her head firmly. "I'm fine, truly. It's just a bruise. Let's get Ana out of this place."

I exhale a long sigh of relief. Ana and Camille are safe.

As we head out into the corridor, several of my men pass us. Kat keeps a protective arm around Ana's face, shielding her from the mayhem. We head to the stairs, carefully stepping over broken frames and debris, bullet casings, and shattered furniture. The smell of smoke and blood is overpowering.

At last, we reach the ground floor, stepping into the once-grand foyer. Doors hang off twisted hinges, splintered wood and glass lay everywhere. The fight is done, but the cleanup is far from over.

Just outside the kitchen, a make-shift triage has been set up. Vlad is there on a stretcher, an IV bag hanging next to him, the line set firmly into the thick vein on his hand. I can't believe what I'm seeing, as I thought he would have been well on his way to the hospital by now.

Camille hovers next to him for a brief moment, then gently rubs Ana's back. "Come with me, hmm?" she whispers to her. "Let's get you some fresh air."

Ana hesitates, glancing at Kat. Kat nods, gently transferring her to Camille, shielding her view of Vlad. "Stay close," she tells them both.

As they head toward the terrace, I focus on Vlad. Kat bends over him, gripping his uninjured hand. "Are you okay?" she asks.

He winces as he offers a weak smile. "Been better," he croaks.

Sergei, one of the medics, a burly man with a kind face, tapes fresh bandages over his shoulder wound. "He was lucky," Sergei says. "The bullet passed through his shoulder clean. He's lost a lot of blood, and he has several broken ribs. We're going to take him to the hospital in a few minutes."

Kat bows her head, pressing her forehead to Vlad's good hand. "You'll be alright," she insists, voice quivering. He closes his eyes, nodding faintly.

Sergei motions to me. "We need to move him STAT. He needs proper treatment."

"Do it; whatever he needs."

Vlad glances toward me. "You kill that bastard?" he asks.

"Piotr's gone," I confirm grimly. "He won't hurt your family again."

He exhales, pain flickering across his face. "Good."

Kat kisses Vlad's forehead before the medics wheel the stretcher into the elevator. Kat moves to follow, but I catch her arm.

She stiffens. "I want to go with him."

"You'll see him soon," I say softly, "but we need to gather ourselves first, Kat. Then we'll meet him."

Nikolai appears, wiping blood from his brow. "We're still scanning the place. No more hostiles found. Piotr's men are either dead or gone." His gaze dips, noting Kat's tear- and blood-streaked face. "Vlad's going to be okay," he adds, more gently. "One of my men had already called the paramedics when you ordered him taken to the hospital. They were here by the time we got him downstairs. They wanted to stabilize him before transporting him.

"Boss, we can wrap things up. You and your family should get out of here, go to a nice hotel or something."

Kat nods, relief and sorrow colliding in her expression. "Yes, please."

I slip an arm around her. "Piotr's body is in the office," I say quietly to Nikolai. "Bury it in an unmarked grave. He doesn't deserve anything more."

Kat tenses beside me but she doesn't protest. She's mourning the brother she once knew, not the monster he'd become. Nikolai bows his head, stepping away to handle it.

We grab Camille and Ana and take the elevator downstairs. A swirl of night air greets us when we step outside. The courtyard is lit by the headlights of several black SUVs, our personal medics milling around with first-aid kits, taking care of any injuries, Nikolai's team mans the perimeter, weapons still at the ready.

No police—they know better than to interfere in Bratva business.

Camille stands to one side, holding Ana in her arms. My child gazes at us, eyes puffy, face streaked with tears and exhaustion. My heart clenches. Damn! I wish she didn't have to witness any of this. I vow to myself that, going forward, she never will again.

Kat approaches them, wrapping them both in a hug. Camille glances at me. "What about Vlad?"

"He's on his way to the hospital," I say. "We'll join him soon."

Kat cups Ana's cheek, smoothing away tears. "You okay, baby?"

Ana nods weakly. "Tired," she murmurs.

Kat gently kisses her temple. "We'll get you somewhere you can sleep, sweet girl. It's all over now."

I slip my hand on Kat's shoulder. "We should get going."

She gives a longing glance at the building before letting me guide her toward one of the waiting vehicles. I help her get Ana settled and buckled in on her lap in the back seat.

Camille climbs in next to them, wrapping her arm around them protectively. I slide into the passenger seat, nodding at the driver—one of Nikolai's men.

"Go," I instruct, voice rough with fatigue.

He drops it into drive. As we pull away from the battered remains of the building, I catch a glimpse of bodies being dragged out, Piotr's among them, presumably. A wave of heaviness presses on my chest. He was family to Kat and Vlad, once a friend to me, but he shattered those bonds. I had no choice.

Kat's humming brings me back. She kisses Ana's hair as Camille strokes her arm. Leaning back in the seat, I release a heavy sigh. We're alive. Vlad's alive. The threat is gone. Now we just have to piece our lives back together.

Ana exhales her own sigh as she drifts off. I rest my head against the seat, letting my eyes close for a moment. My thoughts swirl with images of bullet-riddled halls, Vlad bleeding out, Piotr's final glare before I fired. My eyes pop open as I cling to a single truth—we're alive.

Whatever tomorrow holds—Vlad's recovery, the city's reaction, the burial of a brother who died a traitor—we'll endure it. Kat's hand reaches out for mine. I squeeze it gently, letting the warmth of her grip steady me. We're together, and we're free of Piotr's dark ambitions.

We're safe.

That's enough for now.

EPILOGUE I

KAT

One week later...

I stand by the casket as light drizzle begins to fall. The day is grey, fitting for a funeral.

Though Pavel had wanted Piotr to be buried in an unmarked grave, we knew that wasn't the right thing to do. We need to keep up appearances in order to avoid any further fighting. So here we are, pretending.

Everyone in attendance—from low-level enforcers to high-ranking Bratva figures—wears an expression of forced sympathy and tense politeness. They were told Piotr died in a hunting accident.

It's a convenient lie, one that won't raise too many questions. No one wants to unravel the possibility that we turned on our own family. If they suspect foul play, they keep it to themselves.

The headline in the media read: *Andreev Pakhan Meets Tragic Fate in Upstate Woods.*

According to unofficial rumors, it was a misfire or perhaps a stray bullet from another hunter. We didn't bother specifying details. No one wants an open scandal. The only men who know the truth are dead or bound to secrecy by loyalty to Pavel, Vlad, or me.

I glance at my brother's sealed coffin, resting on a small platform draped in black cloth. My heart wrenches, and I swallow back the bitter taste of bile rising in my throat. Even though I hated what Piotr became, a part of me still mourns the little boy who used to tug at my pigtails and hide frogs in my shoes.

A swirl of conflicting emotions churn in my chest—anger, heartbreak, relief—and I can't decide which one is the strongest.

On my right, Pavel stands tall, projecting authority in his tailored black suit. He stays quiet, simply nodding at those who express condolences. Surrounding us are several members of the Fetisov Bratva, all wearing neutral expressions, offering subdued gestures of respect.

On my left, Vlad leans on a cane, courtesy of the beating our departed brother gave him. He insisted on attending the funeral ceremony on his own two feet.

"Don't treat me like an invalid," he'd snarled when I suggested a wheelchair.

Camille helps him stay balanced, her hand discreetly under his elbow, her gaze never leaving him for long.

Vlad's face is still bruised; purplish shadows mar his cheekbones, but they're mostly hidden beneath his dark sunglasses. His broken ribs and contusions are slowly healing. I know he's in pain, but stubbornness and sheer determination keep him going.

Ana stands between Pavel and me. My daughter hasn't left my side since the day everything exploded. She's clinging to my hand with a grip so tight it numbs my fingers.

At only five, she doesn't fully grasp the tragedy behind this funeral. All she knows is that the uncle she adored has died, and she doesn't understand why. She sniffles, tears slipping silently down her cheeks. She thinks it was a real accident, that her Uncle Piotr was the victim of misfortune in the woods. One day, when she's much older, maybe I'll explain what really happened, but not now.

Let her grieve a simpler lie.

A hush descends over the small crowd gathered around the casket. Viktor Novikov emerges from behind a cluster of men, stepping forward with measured solemnity. Drizzle speckles his black overcoat; droplets shine on his broad shoulders. He's flanked by a pair of silent associates.

Novikov bows his head to Vlad and me, a show of respect as hollow as it is necessary. "My condolences," he says plainly. "Piotr's death is a loss to the entire community."

I manage a tight nod, forcing politeness I don't feel. "Thank you for coming," I say, ignoring the bitter taste in my mouth. Novikov is probably attending only to ensure he's not being blamed for anything. His presence is a power move, an attempt to save face. He knows Piotr's death means that we now hold both Andreev and Fetisov power. If anything, he's the one walking on eggshells now.

Pavel steps forward, shaking Novikov's hand. One of us has to be diplomatic, I suppose. "We appreciate your support," he says. "It means a great deal that you have come to pay your respects."

Novikov nods, chancing a quick look at Vlad. Vlad ignores him, focusing on a point in the distance. He's still seething under the surface—Piotr's back-door alliance with Novikov nearly destroyed us all.

Vlad limps forward on his cane, careful not to overstrain his injured shoulder and broken ribs. "Viktor," he says in a low voice. "We should meet tomorrow."

The new *pakhan* of the Andreev Bratva has made a request. There's no *should* about it.

Novikov's expression wavers, uncertain. "Tomorrow?"

"Yes," Vlad repeats. "You and I have matters to resolve." He doesn't elaborate, but the tone of his voice and his threatening stance, despite the cane, gives a clear message: *Don't try double-crossing my family again.*

Novikov can probably sense how precarious his position is now. He nods in agreement. "Of course," he says, stepping back. "I'm available at your convenience." Then, Novikov returns to the crowd of mourners; his men follow.

The entire scene feels so surreal—Piotr's casket in front of us and a scattering of men from various Bratvas offering stilted condolences.

We stand in the Andreev family cemetery plot, a small garden of stone markers and weeping willows. Camille stands close to Vlad, her hand clutching his.

Ana tugs on my hand, her voice quivering. "Mama can we go now? I don't like it here."

I slide my palm over her damp curls. The drizzle has picked up, turning into a light rain. "Soon, *petite etoile*," I promise.

The ache in my heart intensifies, guilt gnawing at me. She's so young to be facing so much loss. She loved her uncle. He was always kind to her, at least on the surface. I exchange a glance with Pavel, silently asking if we can wrap this up. He nods, reading my discomfort. We murmur our last respects near the casket, gather our immediate circle, and step away.

The handful of watchers part to let us pass, bowing their heads. Viktor Novikov pretends to ignore our departure, though I can feel his sharp gaze on our backs.

We climb into the waiting car—a sleek black sedan assigned to us for the day, its windows tinted. Pavel slides into the front passenger seat, giving instructions to the driver. Vlad, with Camille's help, eases into the back seat. I settle in beside him, and Ana clambers onto my lap, not wanting the slightest space between us. The driver slowly rolls away from the cemetery. The tension in my chest eases a little bit, and I let out a small sigh of relief. I hate funerals, especially when they're for family under conditions of secrecy and half-truths.

Ana sniffles, pressing her face to my collarbone. "Mama," she mumbles, "Uncle Piotr's not coming back, is he?"

My stomach twists. I brush a hand through her curls. "No, baby. He's gone."

She nods miserably, a small sob escaping. "I don't understand," she whispers. "He said he loved me. Why would he leave—" She can't even finish the sentence, too confused and hurt.

I exchange a quick, pained look with Pavel, who turns around from the front seat. His eyes soften, but there's no easy explanation.

I stroke Ana's back, my heart heavy. "He did love you, in his own way," I say carefully. "Sometimes, grown-ups make terrible mistakes. But he wouldn't want you to worry or be sad, I promise."

I'm not sure if that's the right answer. My gaze flicks to Vlad, who's leaning his head against the seat, eyes closed.

The rain intensifies, hammering against the car roof. We drive in an uneasy hush, the city's silhouette blurred by the downpour. Eventually, we reach the old family estate on Long Island, where we'll be staying while Pavel's building is being repaired.

Gunfire and violence tore our home to pieces, and I can't bear the idea of living there again until it's completely restored, every inch repaired and updated. We've spent the last week in a luxury hotel, but Ana needs something more stable.

We pull through the estate gates, the driver parking near the front steps. A handful of loyal men guard the house. Security has been doubled after everything that happened. Vlad stirs, wincing as he tries to sit up straighter.

Camille helps him out of the car. I linger, letting Ana slip from my lap. She rubs her eyes. "I'm tired," she says, her voice small.

I get out and take her hand. "Let's get you inside and tucked in." She nods gratefully, clinging to my side as we head up the steps. I can't help but notice the chipped paint, the neglected shrubs.

Piotr never cared for the estate, and his mismanagement has taken its toll.

Inside, it's warm, though the halls feel hollow. Memories of my parents and my life here as a child come flooding back—a younger me running through these corridors, Piotr shouting after me to slow down. I grit my teeth, swallowing back the swirl of emotions.

We must push forward.

Pavel lingers to talk briefly with the security detail who followed in another car, discussing updated measures. Vlad and Camille vanish to find a place where he can lie down. I take Ana to an upstairs bedroom—my old room—once upon a time.

The wallpaper is faded lilac, and I recall how I used to hate it. Now, however, it feels oddly comforting. Thankfully, the staff already visited, leaving us some fresh linens and tidying up just a bit.

Ana rubs her nose, glancing around. "Is this your room, Mama?"

"Used to be," I say, pulling down the comforter. "It's not super cozy right now, but we'll make it work, okay?"

She nods, exhaustion weighing on her face.

"You won't leave me, right?" she asks. The tremor in her voice makes my heart crack.

I kiss her forehead. "I'll stay until you fall asleep," I promise. "But I'll be close by."

She sniffles. "Okay." In less than a minute, her eyes flicker shut, the day's sadness pulling her under. I stroke her hair gently, waiting until her breathing evens out.

My chest tightens with immense love for her, sorrow for the illusions she lost. She doesn't know the full truth, and for now, that's best. Pavel and I will decide down the road if it's something we want to tell her.

I wait a while after she falls asleep before slipping out, carefully easing the door shut. In the hallway, I press a shaky hand over my mouth, fighting back the tears that threaten to fall.

Stay strong, Kat. Your family needs you.

I wander down the corridor. My old bedroom is just around the corner from my parents' old suite. The entire second floor feels like a memory that doesn't belong to me anymore.

Eventually, I find Pavel in what used to be my father's office, rummaging for something amid dusty bookshelves. He glances up, relief washing over his face when he sees me.

"Hey," he says gently. "Ana okay?"

I nod, hugging myself. "She's asleep. Had to promise I wouldn't go far."

He sets aside a stack of old paperwork, stepping toward me. "I can't blame her for being anxious. She's been through hell."

My throat thickens. "We all have. I'll check on Vlad soon, make sure Camille got him settled. He looked ready to pass out in the car."

Pavel slides an arm around my waist then raises my hand to his lips, kissing it, a tender gesture that makes me release a breath I didn't realize I was holding.

"We'll make sure he's okay. We'll make sure everyone's okay. Peace will be restored, and we won't have to worry anymore." Then, with a slight bend of his knee, he leans down and kisses my belly.

A swirl of fear, gratitude, and love takes over. I rest a hand on his shoulder, letting the warmth of his presence ground me. "You really believe we'll have peace after this?"

He straightens, pushing a stray curl behind my ear. "We're merging the Fetisov and Andreev Bratvas, forging a united front. Novikov sees our strength—he's not going to risk an all-out war now that Piotr's out of the way. Once Vlad recovers, we'll confirm alliances. Yes, there will be bumps, but it'll be better than constant betrayal."

I allow a tiny smile. "You're sure?"

His dark eyes soften. "I'll do whatever it takes to protect you, Kat. You, Ana, and our baby. That's my priority. That will always be my priority."

I slip my arms around his neck, pressing my face to his collar. "I trust you," I say. "I mean it."

He draws back slightly, studying me, then he leans in and kisses me. My pulse flutters. "I love you."

A smile curves his lips. "I love you, too." He kisses me again. My thoughts drift to the future.

We'll bury the old illusions about Piotr, bury the brutality he wrought. We'll rebuild our home and salvage the happy memories there. Ana deserves that. She deserves a loving, joyful childhood without danger or fear clouding it.

Pavel's hand drifts down, pressing against my belly in a protective gesture. "No more secrets," he says.

Before he even says the words, I know what he's referring to.

"With Ana, either."

"We'll tell her when she wakes up."

His eyes shine with a quiet sort of joy on a day that's held so much grief. He leans down, brushing his lips to my forehead.

"Let's do it together."

I take his hand.

Together.

I wouldn't have it any other way.

EPILOGUE II

PAVEL

Eight months later...

"You've got this. Just breathe—slow and steady."

Kat's fingers clamp down on mine like a vise, and I wince. I've handled gunfights, ambushes, and high-stakes negotiations without breaking a sweat, but watching her go through labor knocks the breath out of me.

She turns her head, eyes blazing despite the exhaustion.

"Pavel," she grits out between contractions. "I love you to pieces, but if you tell me to breathe one more time, I swear—"

Another contraction seizes her, cutting off whatever threat she was about to issue. I rub her back, feeling completely useless, but desperate to do something.

The nurses in the room are infinitely calmer than either of us, and they coach her through each step. "You're doing amazing, Mrs. Fetisova. Just a little more."

Amazing? My wife is a damn warrior.

Kat screams, throwing her head back as she gives one last push. Time slows, stretching out with unbearable tension, and then—a sharp, furious wail shatters the room.

My lungs finally start working again. The nurses check him over. The second they place our son in Kat's arms, my whole world narrows down to one moment.

Kat, exhausted, stares at him like he's the greatest thing.

And he is.

He's tiny, with a wrinkled little face that's absolutely perfect.

My chest tightens with something fierce and familiar, similar to what I felt when I found out Ana was mine. Love, of course, but bigger, heavier, a responsibility I never knew I was capable of holding.

Kat glances up at me, her lips curling into a tired smile. "We made this."

I laugh. "We did."

The baby lets out another little cry. I let go of Kat's hand to gently brush a fingertip across his soft forehead. He's so small, so delicate, but at the same time, he's everything.

"We still haven't picked a name," Kat points out, stroking his tiny back.

We've spent months going back and forth, shooting down each other's suggestions, never quite settling on anything. But looking at him now, I know.

"I think I have one," I say, clearing my throat. "Mikhail."

Kat's eyes widen, fresh tears welling up. "My father's name?"

I nod. "He should have something of his grandfather's, something of both families."

She presses her lips together, cradling our son closer. "Mikhail Andreev Fetisov," she whispers, testing it out. Then she looks at me, her expression soft and loving. "It's perfect."

"Yes," I say, leaning in to kiss her temple, then the tiny bundle in her arms. "Just like him."

The baby makes a slight noise as he settles against Kat's chest, his tiny fingers curling. I watch him, completely lost in the moment.

We've fought for this—through hell and back. And now, finally, we have something untouched by all the violence, all the pain.

We have him.

She gives me a tired smile. "I love you," she whispers, breath catching on the last word.

I set my forehead against hers.

"I love you," I echo.

Kat sniffles, then laughs, brushing away fresh tears as she gazes down at Mikhail. "He's...he's just so...perfect," she says, and I couldn't agree more.

A nurse steps forward, offering a gentle smile. "We need to do a few quick tests, all routine, but we can do everything right here."

Kat hesitates, arms instinctively tightening around Mikhail. I squeeze her hand, reassuring her.

"He'll be okay. We can watch the whole time."

She exhales slowly and nods, allowing the nurse to take our son to a small station on the other side of the room.

I stay by Kat's side, my eyes glued to Mikhail as they weigh him, check his tiny limbs, and clean him up.

His soft cries tug at my heartstrings, but the nurse hums soothingly, working with practiced hands.

The quiet doesn't last long. A soft knock at the door makes us both look up. Ana peeks inside, her eyes wide with excitement.

"Mama? Papa?"

My heart still stumbles at the word Papa. She's called me Papa for months now, but hearing it in this moment, as she steps into the room to meet her baby brother, feels like something sacred.

"Come here, sweetheart," Kat says, her voice thick with emotion.

Ana rushes inside, her little legs carrying her straight to the bed. Vlad follows close behind, looking strong and steady, a far cry from the battered man he was months ago. Camille is beside him, a loving smile on her lips as she watches Ana climb up onto the bed with Kat's help.

Ana's eyes go wide as she takes in the empty blanket where the baby should be. She frowns.

"Where's my brother?"

Kat brushes a hand over her hair. "The doctors and nurses are just checking him over. See?" She points across the room where Mikhail is being carefully wrapped in a fresh blanket, a tiny diaper covering his bottom.

Ana considers this, then nods seriously, as if weighing the importance of medical procedures. "Okay. But I want to see him first next time."

Vlad chuckles, ruffling her curls. "I'm sure we can arrange that, little lady."

Camille perches on the edge of the bed, watching Kat with fondness. "You did amazing," she says. "And look at you—already glowing and still beautiful after just giving birth. It's almost unfair."

Kat snorts, wiping at her tired eyes. "Liar. I look like I just went to war."

Camille grins. "And you won."

Before Kat can reply, the nurse turns to us, smiling. "All good. He's healthy and strong." She carefully lifts Mikhail, bringing him back over and placing him in Kat's waiting arms.

Ana gasps. "He's so little," she whispers in awe.

Kat laughs softly. "You were this little once, too."

Ana's eyes widen as if that's the most unbelievable thing she's ever heard. Then she wiggles closer, her tiny hands resting carefully on the edge of Kat's blanket.

"Can I hold him, Papa?"

I nod; my throat tight with emotion. "Of course, baby girl. But you have to sit down first."

I lead Ana over to the guest chair then go back over to Kat. Carefully, she shifts Mikhail into my hands. Ana waits with open arms. I place Mikhail in her lap, supporting his head and explaining how to hold him, keeping my hands underneath hers for extra support. Camille presses a hand to her chest, beaming, as Vlad lets out a quiet chuckle.

"Look at you," he murmurs, squeezing Ana's shoulder. "Already the best big sister."

Ana's face lights up at the praise. "I'll protect him," she promises, her voice fierce, matter-of-fact, and full of love.

I slide an arm around Kat's shoulders, pressing a kiss to her temple. She leans into me, her hand resting over mine as we watch our family—the one we fought for, bled for, and built from the ashes of everything we lost.

Our family, whole and safe, finally stepping into the life we've built, the future we're building.

"I think you can take him back now," Ana says. Laughter fills the room.

I walk over and carefully take my son from Ana's little arms then head back to Kat. "Welcome to the world, Mikhail," I whisper, leaning in to kiss the top of his head. Kat squeezes my hand, and as I look into her tear-bright eyes, I know we've finally found our happily ever after.

Vlad clears his throat, smirking. "So, when's the next one?"

Kat groans, but I just laugh, pulling her closer. "Let's enjoy this one first."

For now, the rest of the world can wait. All that matters is this moment, and the family we've become.

THE END

Printed in Dunstable, United Kingdom